PORTFOLIO | *milieu*
2004

PORTFOLIO | *milieu*
2004

edited by:
Ingrid Rose
Arleen Paré
Christine Leclerc
Morgan Chojnacki

milieu press
Vancouver, British Columbia

PUBLISHED BY MILIEU PRESS

milieu press
c/o 2559 William St.
Vancouver, BC Canada
V5K 2Y3
www.milieupress.net

Distributed by:
Sumach Press
1415 Bathurst St.
Suite 202
Toronto, ON Canada
M5R 3H8
www.sumachpress.com

Canadian Cataloguing in Publication Data

Portfolio milieu 2004 / edited by Ingrid Rose ... [et al.].

ISBN 0-9733337-1-5

   1. Canadian literature (English)—Women authors.
2. Canadian literature (English)—21st century. I. Rose, Ingrid
PS8235.W7P67 2004   C810.8'09287   C2004-903428-6

Edited by: Ingrid Rose
         Arleen Paré
         Christine Leclerc
         Morgan Chojnacki

Cover Artwork by Cheryl Sourkes
Cover Design by www.mercurygraphics.net
Cover Production overseen by Christine Moore
Typeset and Interior Design by Vancouver Desktop
Printed and bound in Canada by Hignell Book Printing

CONTENTS

most writers need to be read; without an audience the natural cycle of their creative process is incomplete and leaves a certain discomfort under the ribs. what if the kind of writing you do has insufficient outlets? a condition difficult to digest. as a collective of eight women writers— Morgan Chojnacki, Kim Clarke, Christine Leclerc, Christine Moore, Arleen Paré, Shauna Paull, Ingrid Rose, Betsy Warland—we felt hungry for a milieu where voices too infrequently heard (often because they do not fit into identifiable genres) be given space.

to get the range of cutting edge writing by canadian women across canada and elsewhere, *milieu* put out a call for works-in-progress by emerging to established writers of poetry, creative non-fiction and lyric prose. we planned to feature 10-15 selections to give a substantial feel of each individual work as well as the diversity of current writing. the number and quality of manuscripts we received made it clear we would have enough material to publish several different books. *milieu* ended up choosing 21 contributors. four of us worked on this final selection to create the anthology you're now holding.

an anthology of women's writing at this stage of the game! is it necessary? ultimately that's a question each individual reader has to answer for themselves. certainly we felt the need; the response we received indicated a resounding echo among other women writers whose manuscripts seem to have less and less of an opportunity to leave their portfolios; women's presses and bookshops are disappearing, yet women's lives are blossoming with a whole new variety of expression in all the arts.

this collection of writing is filled with the feisty humour and pain of people whose history has been discounted, homelands regained, (in)flagrant odes to language and pasts usurped by the dominant culture, haunting images of the mother lost, the transparent child's experience of the adult world; from the liturgical and the political to the lyrical and the personal.

we interacted with all these for many months and as we became increasingly familiar with them, we were delighted to watch each one find its place in PORTFOLIO *milieu* 2004.

Ingrid Rose, Arleen Paré, Christine Leclerc and Morgan Chojnacki

inventory

inventory

"She made a list of all the wild, immoral things she was too timid,
unwilling, or old to do."   Amy Gestler, *Crown of Weeds*

She made a list of all the things
she was afraid of

yet she was hesitant
the language that filled her was tasteless
slack in the middle of her breakfast
leaving her words
all bone and sinew
a few dry consonants
and a whole lot of bland vowels

and without fresh vowels
she was afraid to choke on her consonants
suffocate on her own humming

yet, she was hungry
and desperate without vowels
but she improvised
deep fried each dread
dusted with icing sugar

                                              ate them with tea

excited, she made a list of what was left over
sorted them into piles
of wild, immoral, and unwilling laundry

carted the unwilling off to thrift stores
cut the wild and immoral into tiny squares, triangles and strips
pieced them into quilt blocks
designs of Drunkard's Path, Swamp Angel, and Memory
then each night she'd undress
roll into their dreamy schemes spread out on her bed
dream like she'd never dreamt before

no grass widow

In one ear I hear Zora Neale Hurston
in my mother's voice,
What are you saying, 'Did I love you?'
Girl, I stayed alive for you
and in the other ear, I hear Elizabeth Brewster
It's fine to be unmarried and childless
that it's enough to be born and not give birth
that I am woman enough
not a white bread spinster
or uppity mooniyawiskwew
thinking she's too good for a poor man or a brown man

I'm no grass widow, but I cut a path with a scythe
as wide as my reach and lace tall sheared stalks
into baskets, not for trinkets, but to bear the weight
of wild wheat heads, millet, black rice,
and mashed berries that bleed into our stomachs
so we can eat for another day

nomenclature

"We know the history of self-exile/ we have begged ourselves too often/ not
to know the truth."

"Waiting for a Friend," Simon Ortiz, *Out There Somewhere*

Surely those who have had their history not so much denied as ignored
know this self-exile in its recounting like a mantra, of the history of
the settlers, in the settlers of history through their naming of the
countless rivers, lakes, mountains, plants, and animals. The naming
over and over of what pre-existed settlers is really only semantics you
say:

you say, *Canada,*   I say, *Turtle Island*

you say, *squaw,*   I say, *Nokum,*

you say, *General Dumont,*   I say, *cousin,*

you say, *Rupert's Land,*   I say, *home,*

you say, *treason,*   I say, *self defence.*

"Nokum," my grandmother – Cree

The Question

"Knowing about being Indian/ just because/ you're an Indian."
"Essentialism," Simon Ortiz, *Out There Somewhere*

The Question: I can feel it welling up like some patriotic standard; I'm rising to my feet with reverence, and I can feel the question prodding my backbone to stand and salute *My People*. It's swelling in my chest like a breast implant, and I'm rising to *the Question* as if I have the answer for the ten little Indians all standing behind me waiting to do the Tomahawk Chop.

The Question: I know and they know it's coming like tax time, and I can tell by their fawning posture they've been meaning to ask this for years, and they trust I will be the even-tempered and rational-minded-Indian who will finally answer it. I'm sure of it forming like a pimple. Their words so carefully chosen like their dinnerware or hair products.

The Question: I can feel the air tighten around us like a mud facial, then decompress like we're both stepping into the deep-deep-kaakaa-territory of unresolved disputes among nations and I, at the border crossing am a Customs Agent who inquires: "Do you have anything to declare?"

my breasts are sensible

like a good pair of walking shoes
they are not nubs on a log
nor are they bulbous peonies
they don't get in the way
when I do chin-ups
nor do they take on their own life
when I run and men don't look
at my chest before they look at my face
my breasts are the size of large oranges
just the right size
for cupping in a hand
offered to my lover like fruit
only occasionally have I
wished for larger ones but
that would throw my whole body
out of proportion and I'd end up looking like
one of those badly pruned evergreens

no, my breasts are sensible.

blind spot

since you left   I have learned not to laugh at characters in dramatic
irony,
    I avoid writing betrayal into anyone's character

despite my age
I was willing to believe in the magic of deft hands
I was willing to believe a woman could be sawed in half
and still walk off the stage

so, let's not call it anything but
betrayal
now that I have trouble spelling it
and spend time
falling backward in regret
of my absentminded ardour
the shear error of my blind spot
the rear-view mirror
and the side mirror
did not reflect you
as small as you really are

my life, a sweet berry

go make friends with this place   this place where you see   both a single
strand of grass bent white in spring and your own soundless sliver of a life
recalled in the lodge-pole pine's slender sway   stirring the sky   bluer
than suede   the wind's mouth warm and smelling of pine rehearsing
summer   imaging itself   the sound of swift water

this first generous day of sun   began forty years ago   when you picked
wild strawberries with you mother   who took a rare break from the
stifling cook shack only to have you stick a berry up your nose
cutting short her only afternoon of leisure   unable to loosen it you
whimpered then wailed back to camp   scrappy as a cat given a bath
you embattled her with your stick arms and legs and she with a tweezers
crouched ready   pushed your skinny twigs away and aimed for the centre
of your face your head thrashing on the cook shack table, mimicking
strangulation   your mother with manual precision   gripped the
attacking berry   spared you suffocation by edible pulpy mass   and now
as you are filled with the song-rush of memory   and the seduction of
nostalgia or worse the conventions of your genre to reconstruct your past
as a sweet berry but, you are rescued from conceit   and this time   it's
not your mother but your own hand   and that damn germ of recall

a thousand scraps of paper

"the derelict bum/ seems to have a universe/ of oddities folded, wrapped,
stashed/ in his filthy bag:/ his tireless attention/ to a thousand scraps of paper"
James Tate, *Selected Poems*

the bag lady that pushes a cart with her bevy,
is not unlike a poet,
her cart like my filing cabinet
is a way of sustaining
a taxonomy of meaning
and it's likely her cart is better organized

she guards her papers with the same passion
as I guard mine
and if by chance some item goes missing
we are equally distraught in locating it
her concern like mine is property: intellectual or otherwise

yet the difference, you argue, is in our quality of life
when sometimes as a poet
I survive no better than she
and most years we both
drag from place to place
what we might need some day:
a thousand scraps of paper

Sunday Solitaire

Sunday evenings loomed like thunderheads
when work would take you
and I was babysat
by Uncle Slim who looked like
he was born in a flap-cap and suspenders
a childless bachelor
generations away

betrayed by your leaving, I pretended
I didn't hear the sound
of footsteps disappearing
down the wooden walkway
every step a heartbeat
at the end of a breath

tempted to bolt after you mewling
I'd hear the truck's door yawn open
your duffle bags drop
in the box of the pick-up
the door's slamming shut
the truck starting
and backing away
gravel snapping under tires
as you pulled away
then the sound between
nothing but
uncle Slim's Solitaire
cards slapping the kitchen table
the slow measurement of time

Do not write for the Harleys

remember the ghosts of past readings?
they are not meek
they will not shrink when you howl
they will merely find a seat
at a safe distance
and observe
they will not disrupt the audience
they will make faces
look cross-eyed, flip their eyelids
or pick their teeth and stare out the window
look deadpan when you crack a joke
so you crack another
but that will only make them search for more lint
or continue their cell phone conversations

there is no greater sense of insignificance
than when a group of junior high students
play tag while you read

but, ahhhhh
these are the things that Literature brings you
but do not submit to the ghosts of past readings
to countless doors that slam shut while you read
or the babies that cry
or the Harleys that rev past

no, do not write for the air conditioners, the fans that beg for repair
the cars without mufflers
the fire alarms or sirens

do not write for the hard of hearing
for you'll snap your vocal chords
screaming your quatrains into their face

no, do not write for the microphones that turn everything you say into
audible slush
the cell phones, the fans, the Harleys
do not write for the sonic boom, cash registers or espresso machines

and especially
do not write for the fans who
come only to hear their favourite poem
and leave pissed because they didn't
you, pop star
you

ALONG THE RIPPLED ROAD

Eyes underwater, she floats past the blunt mist
she no longer tastes. I grip the tide of her bed,
fasten the blue smock that billows from hollow ribs—
a riptide, a shipwreck. How the hull still heaves.

A year ago, less than, my mother took her departure. She left barely a ripple in the sanitized sheets where hunger pooled in her sunken chest. Her eyes held neither word nor cup. When she returned to sea, I journeyed inland, tarried in small spaces, rocked to sleep in the back berth of a white truck headed 240 kilometres northeast of Delhi. Tossed about on the rutted road, my eyes adrift. Afternoon lift. My body ricochets left to right, up and down we swerve to dodge the spill of landslides. The truck lurches, intractable as an ox. I grip the ceiling and pray to reach Lohajan soon.

Amit perches up front with the driver, his plume, a red felt beret tilted at a jaunty angle. At 28, he is already an experienced mountaineer from Bombay. He turns toward me, jostling in the back seat with Nisha and Karthik. A bushy moustache burdens his upper lip, the thick brush ripening his already mature face. Deep creases fold around his mouth to the curve of his cheeks. I trace the fine deep grooves again and again as he speaks. Imagine climbing them.

Amit delivers English instruction in a grave tone that veers, suddenly, almost to the edge of argument. He plants each vowel firmly before placing the next; each phrase clamped tight before fastening another. I brace against the spill of consonants, as ill-fitting phrases twist, writhe, retreat from his lips. As he struggles for meaning.

But when hindi arises, soft as evening prayer, his words bubble bright as onion badji. I await each sound— warm, eucalyptine, bursts like cardamom from a saag paneer. Amit's mouth flavoured with cumin, clove, garlic, carries me over mud pit and tumbling shale. His words mount as we wind west, phrases pile high on a silver palate, his hands glistening in air while I am all fingers and forked-tongue. *Her eyes held neither word nor cup.* My words, an isolated sphere, while meaning streams from his onion mouth—oval, oracle, an opening—his mahogany eyes darting after every detail: *Do you need a rest stop Lorrri?* His rolling rrrrs toppling out along the rippled road.

Amit is restive, except

quietly he hums then opens into a lush, smooth baritone. Sentimental lyrics drift from his tongue, the rumbling vibrato sending the shiver of Shiva stirring along my spine. Mile after mile he croons a hopeful lilt. We lift, pitch, rumble, rise, repeat. But when the radio blasts Bollywood beach music, Nisha, Karthik, Amit and the driver join to belt out the familiar chorus. I drum my fingers on the door handle—the fifth Beatle.

Drum, rumble, ripple, rise, repeat.

Nisha's slender face falls on Karthik's soft shoulder; he cradles her in a swathe of arms. The lovers pour over each other

Five careening at noon and then there were two

Karthik tucks her head into the slope of his neck, the way a duck swallows its bill. We swerve, shift, their arms surround. Eyes downcast, I explore the hidden curves a couple makes, how lovers indissolubly bound, journey on

Five careening in sun and then there was one

Alone, I apprehend only distance. Ripple and rise. *All that remains is a crippled cage, her hollow form in my arms.*

For hours the road coils tightly, a dozen wooden huts lean toward me, trail off, scatter into the high hills. Men crowd, encircle our truck. Their sticky heat swarms, stings, as we arrive at Lohajan worn and weary. Nisha, Karthik, and Amit greet the village men. Longing for release, I leap out, throw my backpack over my shoulder, and scramble uphill to our guesthouse.

Months ago these ranges were jagged lines, ripples, mere shadows on a map. I couldn't place myself among them. Now I venture onto solid ground.

Only nothing feels solid.

Children chitter like bluebirds in the mountain breeze. Barefoot boys swoop to earth, scoop a ball, skitter high above the hill paths. Men spark, their faces twisted in debate. Two young girls play cricket using a tree branch as bat; they shuffle along in oversized black leather shoes, laceless and worn at the heel. "*Namaste*," I call when I pass. They tuck turtle-heads under green sweaters, giggling, their branch hands swaying through lime trunks.

The trees are perfumed strangers. Chir pine and beach advance. I grasp everything, perceive—Silence. Like holding midnight in your mouth.

An image forms another dissolves
> in the distance the sad, slow, galloping hills
> are flooded with fingers, ring around rock, forging
> escape routes.
>> These traces, hardly a body, yet—
> the sky blushes azure, peach-grey, now blood-orange
> as horizons unfold the wings of an open book.

Mountains wreathed in mist soften the furrowed
landscape. I leave behind suffering, free myself from
the shape of things: Nisha's hand steadying on his arm.

Her skin draped from a body broken like the wings of an unfinished book.

I rise   *Her eyes held neither word nor cup* Return
                           stunned, shattered *All day she eats air*

          She expelled truths fathomless as secrets.

Alone above the rippled road
        a woman shivers among tree tops,
    counts down
            the long days
                    a riptide, a shipwreck
            she sinks under

His face   her hand   the moon   a cup

full moon in my cup

The wind surrounds me, calls me back.

How wonder slips from the tongue, how it grows lilies where once a shorn trunk lay lifeless across the path, bearded in moss, bearing the stubble of decayed growth. And between the rootless limbs now, a peak of iris. The pain of prying eyes.

Not where you stand but how long you're prepared to stay.

As the sun dips, our trekking group of three has grown: Kuari Ram, a local guide; Guyan, cook and mountaineer; Ashok, assistant cook; and two muleteers, Ohyan Singh and Prem, have joined us. We are now a family of nine plus four restless mules.

Tonight Amit, Karthik and Nisha play cards by torchlight.
I stand on the porch, watch
      the night innocent as a child's arms reaching through galaxies
         alone   above the rippled road
            a shallow breath, held
        so humid I can almost taste the stars.

FOLD

1st Movement (To)

There was no door to speak for
no door to knock upon   I came for you

lighting candles.

from *What Exile This*

Place. A city is a constant crush of noise. But that's all there is, really.
All there is, and all you would want. You know better than to stalk
ideals, there's no nature to speak for and the people, it all comes down
to people. You've entertained the idea of an empty city, quiet streets to
walk along and theatres opening their doors only to you. But that
dream is a horror, and you take some pleasure in deriding the very
thing that you desire.

There's always the quarry, and you wait for dusk, sometimes
nightfall, to cut across the rail lines with your dogs and descend in
among gravel and rock. Here, the city stops at the edge of a
suspiciously frothy stream amid the bent skeletons of trees grappling
with what lies above. The quarry is a cavity of wind beneath a wide
open sky and the moon sometimes. It's the thing that holds you, the
thing that you come for, the thing that makes you stay. It haunts your
insides, and you trust in that fear, because your bones know it better
than your head, and here, the dogs as well are on edge.

If you were to draw a map of your city, it would say little or nothing about where you are. So, to your mother's mother, and when she mutters prayers or admonitions, you wonder, necessarily, how far back she goes, where she ends up, and why must she take you there with her. Some mornings in waking, you cross deserts, scale mountains, move your body insistently across water. It's a long haul to Canada from the old country, and some days you'd rather be done with it, the motion is dizzying and puts you in an indescribable rage. You would walk away from language if you could, cut the very tongue from your mouth if it would untangle your mind. Some might accuse you of linguistic impropriety, languages copulate imprudently in your mouth, leaving telltale stains on your jaw. You lay claim to none of these, each offers a truncated form of expression, makes you into a bastard every time you open your mouth. What *reine Sprache?* The dream of a fool, and you knew it before even speaking. There is great danger inherent in beginnings, and some days no step is worth taking. You spoke your name and the water in your mouth diluted it. So you drown, every time you speak, you drown again.

Where are you in relation to everywhere you have been? You cross bridges when possible, it seems fitting. Would these rivers have you, you wonder. Bridges pull the city apart, cleave it in two, maybe more. This is where you catch glimpses of the earth, where the earth opens itself to you, to anyone who would have it. In winter, when the dam swallows up the water, you walk on the riverbed, touch what drowns.

You started at the end, you didn't realize it but you did. The plane pulled its weight across the sky and you chose one thing over another. You were bloodless then, and filled your mouth full of other people's names. You stood at the confluence of rivers and crossed them again and again, on foot, by train or bicycle. Your own name held no meaning and you gave it freely. Some tore it from your mouth and you said *Good, take it*. Nothing was worth keeping then, and still today, you question the things you hold on to. Is this the meaning you would attribute to History? A litany of beginnings and endings, a series of departures, a battery of false starts.

Before you were born your mother agreed to die, and you left seeking dreams to bring back to her. You thought you were leaving for good, but really, you were merely walking as she would, if she hadn't just up and quit. Memory is a travesty, she agreed to that pact, but by the time you told her so, it was too late. So you boarded a plane and left in search of language, a single word to attach to yourself, maybe even a name. As you crossed the threshold, your mother spilled water at your feet, saying *Reviens*. Your body wasn't your own then, and today? You think the body in terms of sinew and bone, you understand only crevices.

Your mother brought you up an orphan, and you left a bastard. You went as far as you could, but she tugged at you, like a shore line at earth, and parts of you fell away. So in leaving, you brought everything with you and when you reached your destination, the voice of your mother's mother struck like a blow against your head. The city became small then and there was no way of inhabiting it. You climbed into train upon train, criss-crossing your way over the country, but eventually they all brought you back to where you started, with a head full of voices and no language to call your own. You made fists and shook them at the city and its small minds. You choked on the word lineage and spat it up. Your two hands were tied in a tight knot and no sound would come from your mouth. So you got back on your plane and pushed your way through the sky. The water was dry when you arrived and you showed your empty hands to your mother. *Nothing*, you said, but she wouldn't hear of it, and ran in circles around you until she fell to the floor crying *Jamais!* The door was still open, so you left of course, once again, this time in another direction.

You make a list of places. There is some comfort in that. Places you've
been, places you'd like to visit, places you'll never go. You list the
streets of your city, those you take, those you avoid, those you've never
heard of. You note steep inclines, skateable streets, bicycle lanes,
impasses:

Québec
Liverpool
Arthur
Bristol
Toronto
Kent
Dublin
Glasgow
Cork
...

You live in a city of cities. A stone city that dips into rivers, and carves
itself from other places, imagined and known. You say them out loud,
the names, these and others you haven't bothered to write down. You
could be anywhere right now. Instead you're here, pushing the jagged
edge of earth into water. You're waiting to drown.

And what of the beginning anyway? You want to believe in something new, but daily, your belief tears right down the middle, and only ugliness bleeds through. You make a liturgy of darkness and reinvent the city away from its insistent light and blunt shapes. You make the river into something it isn't and invent new smells to come home to. That leaves you nowhere of course, or everywhere at once, and when your city disappears, you know it will appear again, and you are standing as you were, imagining walls and the bodies they defame. You want something you can't have, something that doesn't exist.

Nabebess. A word risen from a hidden cavity of time. The world is a bright flame burning up the desert inside. Certainly, there is evil to speak for, the earth is a repository of greed and unkindness, but the word isn't yours. Who dies against you?

The names of places matter little. You reach back to the face of your mother's mother and a voice hewn from rock. It could be your own. When she climbed down from her hill and the surrounding mountains, she was heavy already, the world appeared to her differently. How many times did she lunge toward the sea? What words hooked into her?

Je prends ton mal. Yes, you think, but you never leave it behind. The old country is maddening only to those from away. You count yourself among these, the *nochrim*. The gift of heritage is a gift to a stranger, an imposition. You wanted things separate, distinct. Now they are falling into one another. You may claim nowhere as home. Not the streets named after cities in the city in which you live. Nor the sea that batters the shore of a place you've never been to, won't ever know. Nor the sounds that tear from the lips of your mother and her mother before her. The words in your own mouth burn a hole in your tongue. *Je suis.* You begin again: *Soy.* Say: *I.* Falter. None of it's true.

Perhaps, then, that is the place from which you run, the light from which you shield your eyes, the name you refuse to claim. Someone sets truth against faith, and you agree unthinkingly to a truce, tracking verities, each of which knocks up against the place where you are, and of course against you, who make demands even you cannot meet. An exacting tongue, someone says, and you concur, cutting words from stone, waiting for water to come. *Le désir*, you say, but you are wrong to invest so much in language, every word a bruise to your jaw and your mother's jaw before you.

    Caught.

    You are prisoner to the *engrenage* of antecedence: *J'étais*. The word catches in your throat, you don't speak it. Instead it pours out of you creating a gurgling soup of bile. Drown, yes, you would drown, if it weren't for the smell pulling up and out of the whirl of places you return to and leave again. There's no word for this, so you say nothing, casting the grey of your eyes against the falling sky.

Paris is an ending place. And France is a nation built on lies (What country isn't?). There, as everywhere, you suppose, bodies burn as easily as paper. Words are merely pretext, but a pretext to what? It is a country that knows no deference, and why should it? Its history is long, in letters as in politics. It is a country looking always over its shoulder, a strange assemblage of brash monuments and hidden, roiling streets, recalling a greater day, a long gone climax that its inhabitants refer to liturgically, and without remorse, a tedious reprise. It is the country par excellence of *l'injure*, little dogs and the machines that pick up after them.

Paris is a beacon and you know it. So does your mother and that's why she sent you. But that was long ago and why bother thinking about it. Now she merely lies in her bed muttering *Jamais* and sometimes *Reviens*, she doesn't bother to greet you at the door. The mezuza hangs from the doorpost by a rusty nail. Of course it is empty of the reglementary scroll, and merely serves as a decorative casing. The wind knocks it against the brick of the house, pulling one thing from another. You catch hold of the echo, wait for it too to break. It is colder than stone, and older even than that.

Ruins.

You count yourself among the lucky. You pray to no one.

A word is an insufficient net cast over a place. The movement of time is as indiscernible as that of water. Centuries fold into one another, languages collapse on the rutted tongues of weary speakers. You look back at nothing: there are words missing. A trail of furrows branches from the foot of an ancient wall through shifting desert sands. The Negev. Another beginning, you think. And nothing to show for it. You want never to have imagined such a place, you want never to have been called upon to envision its walls and their subsequent collapse. You think—thought—that here, where you are, you are safe from every dictate, every nuance, every turn of phrase. The stacks of books on your shelves discredit you, point accusatory fingers. But silence weighs heaviest of all. Your own silence and the silences that precede you.

Again and again, you agree to lose yourself. You drift back, further even, to Saint-Jean de Luz and the Spanish border, but you do not cross it. You are young yet. It is night and you are not sleeping. The moon pushes its light through a window scoring the red tiles underneath. You tip your eyes over the edge, wonder how long until the sea pulls all the houses under. You are naked in this light but it matters little. You begin to disappear into the small scars of your body. They comprise another language, another way of speaking. Some want blood. You want the certainty of skin closed against itself. A marker for pain or its absence or its eventuality or better yet its imminence. A wild cry held up against a dark and moonless place. There are unspeakable languages and your body is your own. These are the rudiments of a tongue foreign even to you. It is a faint blue flame and you cannot touch it. It is inside you. And you admire it even as you curse it. And you own it even as you condemn it. But your small narrow blade cannot touch it, cannot pull it from inside. Your body accumulates the dust of other bodies, and their heat, their heat. For that, there is no word. And as for the faint blue flame, that madness is your very own. It is a white line streaking across skin. It is born of heat, and the desire to drown.

Breath. There is always reason to leave and reason to return. Or is there? You have only ever heard of people walking forward, or standing still. There are lies in these stories, voices break against words as they speak them. Some agree to that version, of moving forward, away. But what of those who are driven, and the places they leave behind? The words in their mouths betray them. *Hija.* A long line of women stalks the sea. They are landlocked.

Breathless.

In her sleep, your mother gasps for air. That is how she breathes.

With her hands like small bodies curled against her breasts, heaving.

UNDER MY TONGUE

green mango

a mango is good orange runny and sweet
sweet so your skin is marinated golden and
fingers and mouth invite another's tongue
to lick, lick, suck, sweet candy. yum.
good on summer days when sweat
makes brown skin sticky, sticky but salty
salty and sweet like chinese take-out
take a red-bathed shrimp and close your eyes
pretend you're a giant eating a curled limb. yum.
those days when you just have to laugh
at each other's faces, all orange and salty
with red-stained mouths, 'cause there's nothing else to do
but maybe lick.

if you go to indiatown or chinatown
look around between stooping bobbing
blackheads, through waving limbs, below raised voices
you see red and yellow and hairy brown
but look for green, round, tapering at the end
nice weight, good to juggle, heavy
not red or yellow or the colour in between. green
hard. between stone and grapefruit
the closer to stone the better, don't let colour deceive you.
i've succumbed to green and just firmness,
skipping open my front door and muttering in glee:

"green mango, green mango, green mango!"
only to peel off skin and see ripe yellow.
so you can't tell, even if it is green and hard,
whether it is a real, authentic green mango
or not.

let those slept-in soft ones warm yellow to red
in their blushing skins
hold these young ones, hard and sincere
place them to your nose,
if you come from a far away place maybe you'll remember it
if not, then remember this is what green smells like,
this is what fresh is, this is another home. you are welcome.
sticky from sap, wash them under running water
peel them gently, as thin-skin as possible
throw the peel over your shoulder—it might spell
the name of your true love—though not in english.

push knife straight down middle white meat.
cut through the still soft seed, wedge the flesh,
dip in salt in sauce or brave it plain
lay it firm, poking tongue, touching teeth. bite
keer-rawp! ker-rawp! crunch, crunch, over and over
until your head is stupefied with crunch, sour, salt,
again and your tongue brightens in attack
and your mouth fills with water and your
ears and mouth are full, teeth a-battle
so all you hear is thick, thick thunder,
banging your eardrum so much so
that it's all you know
                    you know

way blood travels

between/her & me/her&me
blood   gestures   before birth

      how does the body know

                    how does it forget

mother is known for spices for fingers deep plunged in coriander
her chili intense shan flavours magic ginger thumb touches everything

and i'm away in italy before a small gas stove i find myself
nursing her in the stir of pots missing home and the tastes come out
without any remembered instruction suddenly vaguest cooking
techniques appear in my hands measure by instinct fingertip
improvisation of tongue trained in shan burmese thai cooking through
rolls in the mouth   her in my bones urging curried potatoes come out
tomatoes whirl about orange tinged rice and lemon salad
         crisp fried onion flakes fall into
                    bowls

         from my grandmother
 i inherit
   cravings
  for intense sour
         at the age of three she feeds me tart red fruits
        mashed with salt and nampla
    still recall the taste
want green mangoes dipped in salt pickled gooseberries green plums in
  brine

lime in everything

think of sour and mouth

wells

it's true that people crave what they are:

a sweet soul rushes for candies
salt cravers are fascinating
bitter tongues have anger in their heart
and people who turn to sour

are *sour*

first day

a story

point to the map
name the geographical location
                    here or there where is here whereis

                    which alphabet

         am i a child of monsoon heat
         am i a child of mountain sea

it begins when we leave thailand for
canada saves me from povertyanddiseaseandignorance
                    and other fantasies that run in my head
         my first english words
                    oh where oh where is the toilet?

august landing in vancouver
wearing a luxurious winter coat
of orange velveteen
zipped up ready for snow

first day of school is a misunderstanding of yellow
kids on the floor facing the curly-haired teacher
she speaks and a few students leave for their desks
i hear and imagine fin-feathered blue birds on a red tree
suddenly all heads turn at me tiny in a yellow dress
yellow   the teacher said yellow   you can go to your desk
            she doesn't understand she doesn't speak
english   what is she   does anyone know   hello hello
                                (where is the toilet)

following teacher's instructions all the asian kids line up to try their
language on me

not chinese   *are you sure try again*   *nope*
she's definitely not chinese   *are you sure*

one after another they try me
but no one solves me

i remain
a mystery

inword

*

words   bleach me
  tongue breeds

this language
          overwhelms

    without

          i am

          not

*

    gratefulness

    —

  the sea always escapes me

*

i'm a speechless   blank   constrained to smiles
a hole negation devouring smelly brown skin

i'm thin paper face   ghost living for approval
body goes/farang anchors in/all fingers on deck

knuckles white&ready explosive gestures end-stopped
i'm tongue/short & heaving/trained to jump through
play dead/a strait-jacket letter/written too many times

        *

they've civilized you they've tamed you
                            never dream garlic
                            never stink ginger

long-hair quiet

you who were always raging veins anger lit
domestic lips red heaving and split

                    —

               erase

           *

no better than to take the language to bed with you
               wrapped in sluttish sheets

           your tongue between its legs
        raw and dirty in mouth it comes

in you naked it disappears

think you can pick up your language like you pick stones

will you know the words that come to your ears?

as if you can return to a beach
and still find footsteps

under my tongue

is a world which laughs

is an island where grass grows
a million miles high

there is a tree which carries
volcanoes on its branches' very tip
in leaves of parrot colours

under my tongue
rivals the Amazonian rainforest
in its diversity of many strange things

under my tongue
is an immense ocean
which rolls vowels in its waters
and when the waves
hit my teeth
words splash out

beware

under my tongue
is a word
deadly as a dart
that can pierce someone's heart

THE DIVE

I.

Water cool starts at fingertips slicing into surrounding
wet. Every crevice drenched—instantly.

Sudbury is a short map of wilderness to my mother's
brother, who lives in a large shack. No running water.
No electric anything. Down the road my aunt his
exwife lives in the relative luxury of a heated cottage
with an attached outhouse, wellwater running from
her taps. I envy her the warmth but am glad to be
staying at my uncle's—unkempt and wild. My family
a visiting pack.

This is not my first summer here. Not my first dip in
Tilton Lake.

Tilt me on my axis—push me off.

Cousin and Brother walk with me towards our daily
swim. We find the dirt path, the unpaved lane.

i am

With each step savouring the dryness of the air, the moonscapes of alkaline land that have absorbed the ends of the nickel industry built decades before. Wild blueberries grow across shields of rock, spots of earth too parched and tiny for anything else.

My feet know dust in this lane. We walk down its arch as it sweeps towards Circle Road, which surrounds the lake. We cross it then step into a narrow path that leads to the shoreline. To large boulders that start near trees and round out, sinking below the water's (quiet) morning surface.

sorry

This lake knows my name. I know its face. When I tuck myself into its arms, it holds me.

A tide stirs my limbs as I stand on the shore. Brother and Cousin talk behind me, boy voices now deeper at 15. They move to the water's edge, bend down to palm stones and aim towards the lake's heart. Waves rivet my feet to rock.

They throw.

I watch the ripples, feel their edge, cutting on the first bounce, fading into distance.

This is my lake. I know the curves of this body. Want lakes to fill my body, cleanse me of my need to fear things. My fear of needing things.

Father

This flash surges up to my heart. I raise my hands
overhead and bend my knees. Sun hits the water,
blinds me.

                        for not being your sister Beyle

I have been here before. Have seen this spot a hundred
times.

This lake.

I claim it.

In my body.

The scene before my eyes splinters—I freeze as shards
sink into my stomach, chest, throat.

                                        Father

i am nowhere
            in a black hole that never ends
                            falling   i reach out
there are no branches
                                i plunge
breathe black   in

                every moment   slows   heightens
needles in my veins prick my eyes, breath,
                                hearing
every sound
                        every feeling   magnified

black rushes in

i want every moment
            turned down

want it all   *to hold*
                              still

A ring of laughter pulls me back, back to the shore of
Tilton Lake, legs frozen to rock. Cousin and Brother
on my right. I sense their pulse, their vigour.

I want no more of them.

Of anything.

                              i am sorry

I am too awake. Too alive to my body to stand its
encasement.

                    for not being your sister Simha

I push with my legs.

Knowing.

This lake.

Is.

My body.

Feel that moment of being airborne, instant's wind biting cheeks, arms, thighs, feet. Horizontal dive to edge's water.

i am

This lake.

I know.

Her.

My mother.

sorry

My fingers break the surface, spread apart opening her limbs to my body: there is ancient moonrock.

Father

My head parts the water my hands have already touched.

I give myself.

To this.

STONE.

I hear the blow at the top of my scalp.

I leap from my body, watch the ripple along my spine.

My body rips me back to itself as muscles quiver
around my vertebrae. Heart slows.

I want to NOT live.

I want to NOT die.

I want it all to STOP.

Instead, this enormous pain the size of the world seizes
my shoulders, clamps around my neck, obliterates
prior anguishes.

Face in the water, I float: "What if I stay?"

II.

But the water pushes me away. Arms against rock,
knees bend and body rises, stiff. I gulp air, turn, neck
muscles constricted, shoulders locked into place.
Cousin and Brother stand on either side, fear marking
their bodies, their eyes. This lake.

"Are you okay?"

"I heard a crack."

i am sorry

The boulder beneath me sighs and water tucks itself
under my nails and I say, "Have to get back."

"Can you walk?"

I grip Brother on my left, Cousin on my right,
squeezing. Hard. I want to hurt. Cause pain. My skull
vibrates.

"You're hurting my arm."

"Mine too."

I loosen my hold. My cheeks flush as heat shivers
between and up my shoulders. Turns my arms and
fingers cold.

i am not

We walk back up the path, dust clinging between toes.
Over stones and grass to the wood steps of the porch.
Screen door creaks as we walk in.

your brother Anselm

Father looks up. Light from north-facing windows
bathes him in white. An arc of silence curves around
the room.

your father Mikiel

Fear scars his hallowed face. This face I recognize as
my own.

your mother Reyna

A drone in my neck turns to a thrum that fills my legs, arms, belly. I sit down in the chair by the door. Father's eyes turn to ash. He rises, grips his chair.

I swallow. Words work their way up. "I. Hurt my neck. Need. To get to the hospital."

He squints. "Maybe, what, maybe a good sleep." His mouth closes, opens, "After resting . . ."

The body that is mine grips my bones and shakes words from me. "Father. I need to. To go." Quiet breath. "Now."

His fingers are white. "Ach," he coughs, "you're right." He lets go. "Yes. Right of course."

We cram into the car, all seven of us. The motor hums. I hold my breath often. An aching grin flutters across my face, and white heat (of pain) fills me, fuels the lightning rod of a new scar opening up under my ribs. Open to a new truth.

sorry

The car jolts and a bolt sears my legs, strikes my chest: What have I done? A howl in my belly. I shut my eyes. My neck burns, blazes with heat, scalds my heart, its rhythm, slams into my breath. My eyes snap open: What have I left undone?

A hole spreads through me, leaves a tattered circle, empty.

We arrive.

Father stops the car in front of doors with
EMERGENCY printed in red bold above. Neck big
with the fill of a wooden spear, beating in the centre, I
slide from the back seat and step out. I hear a
clambering behind me. I don't wait.

I stride through the glass doors that slip open for me.
A nurse looks up and shouts Wheelchair! She hurries
towards me, takes my arm, starts to orchestrate the
personnel around her. A flurry of movement as she
wheels me (seated in a rolling chair) to a white-cloaked
man labelled Dr. Green.

His unlined face is young, his gaze darts to my neck.
He blinks and chews on his upper lip. Sniffs. Tells me
I need to have x-rays taken.

for this unholy ruin

Mother, Father and family disappear.

this misshapen world

Dr. Green wheels me to a room with grey walls and
machines with metal limbs. A woman labelled X-Ray
comes out from behind a partition, and they help me
lay down on a high surface, face up. His thin fingers
press my left cheek downward against my contracted
neck. My eyes water as my right cheek meets cold
metal FUCK OFF BASTARD HOW DARE YOU?!

X-Ray manoeuvres a huge metal arm above me.
They both disappear.

thrummbmm-click—my frozen limbs absorb the
machine's purr.

                                              dread

Dr. Green returns, his hands turn my other cheek
until a full vibrating numbness seeps into my arms.
X-Ray reappears, moves the metal contraption, leaves
again with Dr. Green.

thrummbmm-click

                                          delivered

Hands at my hips, Dr. Green rolls me to my side, then
stomach, and the woman repositions the instrument
above my neck.

thrummbmm-click

                                  into your first breath

"You can wait with your family 'til we get the results."
He confers with X-Ray.

The Emergency nurse materializes, wheelchair in tow.
She lifts my head gently, wraps a thick foam brace
around my neck, secures it with Velcro. She helps shift

me onto my side. I let my legs swing down, slide into the seat. She wheels me to the waiting room.

Father.

i am sorry

He stands.

"Don't worry," I lick my lips. "I'll be fine."

Father's mouth is a line.

for the pain

Eyes dim, tighten.

embedded under your eyes

I rise and sit in a real chair. He sits next to me. Mother and Sister arrive with tea for everyone. We drink it hot.

Dr. Green returns. He speaks of dislocated vertebrae, of muscular spasm, of the chance that the muscles of my neck, shoulders and back will re-locate my dishevelled spine. "Keep wearing the foam brace, get some painkillers." He turns to Father. "She'll be fine."

pain held

A wave of relief flows through me while my heart spasms regret that I didn't knock myself into further oblivion.

naked

Is this all there is to be? This spike in my neck, and this enormous futility?

III.

In the car everyone chatters around me while my neck grips my body like a fist. Voices rise and fall, edge towards laughter—I wince against their pitch. Father's voice swells at his early assertion that getting a good night's rest would set things right.

A stab penetrates the centre and bottom of my skull, makes my eyes widen.

At the cottage we pile out, my feet find the earth and I make my way inside. Father curses the cottage, Sudbury, the lake. He squints, white shadows beneath his eyes.

i want to brush those hollows away

His breath is ancient thorns. The air fills with them and they waft towards me, seep in.

I sit in a chair, back straight, neck held in place. The sun slips from the room. Mother and Sister light candles and oil-lamps. Brother and Cousin slam the door in a scramble to get wood from the shed.

Cans of sauce crack with the sound of opening. Water bubbles its readiness for noodles, vegetables meet the edge of a knife. Mother and Sister and Uncle move around in the kitchen.

Father sits down with a paper, folded, in his lap. His face white, his eyes fixed on the foam around my neck.

want to reshape the world in your image

He shakes his head, looks towards the window.

reorder decades

Supper prepared, we sit at table, and the savoury scent of sauce over pasta fills my senses.

We eat.

can't

A knock from outside kicks my blood into a driving heat. Uncle moves to the door and I hear Auntie's strong voice a soft rush of words passed to him. My stomach lurches as Uncle returns to table, cracks jokes and asks: "How would you like to stay in a heated room with a TV and electric lights tonight?"

My eyes flit to him as my heart leaps to Dr. Green, his clumsy hands. "What do you mean?" Father asks, staring at him, at me. "The Chief Surgeon at the hospital wants you in for a few days." Uncle continues eating. "You're joking?!" says Father.

"For observation," Uncle chews.

Blood drains from my neck, arms, fingers. Eyes sting.
My chest pounds. The skin under Father's eyes turns a
pale blue.

your need

"I'll be. Fine. Dad, let's go." I push my chair back, heart
thumping. Heat slashes my left cheek, chin, moves under
my breast and drops to the soles of my feet.

Father mutters under his breath.

is louder than my voice

I hear the blood pulse from my chest to my neck, feel
the throb in its core.

IV.

At the hospital. I enter EMERGENCY again. Less
sure of the reason I am here. A man thick across the
shoulders, palms wide, eyes bright, introduces himself
to me: Dr. Powers. He explains that when he reviewed
my case, he decided to have me come back in for a few
days. Just a precaution, he says.

His gaze direct and open, the ache in my neck
subsides.

I am led to a private room and positioned on my back;
my head is placed in gentle static traction and I am
told I should not, will not, move.

For three days.

I sleep.

*

On the first morning, I wake and count the spots on
the ceiling, sleep deeply.

Later, I open my eyes, shift a millimetre right, left.
Practice curling my fingers and toes. Doctors and
nurses and family come and go and I don't pay them
much attention.

I sleep.

*

On the second day Mother stays, tells me news of the
day. Talks of wild blueberries picked yesterday, the pie
she is making, that will be ready for me tomorrow when
I return to the cottage.

She leaves for tea.

Father

He comes in, approaches the bed. I stare at him. "Hey
Dad," I say. He shakes his head, "Goddamn." He
looks down above my head, at the steel that keeps me

in place. "Can't believe this . . ." The skin under his eyes loses colour.

your need

He shakes his head.

is stronger than my will

"Dad. No. I will. I'll be fine."

My heart speeds up.

I am not afraid.

I tell him.

My body feels strangely buoyant. Light with the feeling of not needing to do anything but be still.

i love you first

He puts a hand against my cheek, smoothes my hair back. He nods, "Yes. I know. You'll be f . . ." His eyes well up.

I feel a ripple of energy move away from my spine, a tinge of malice quiver on my face and in my bones.

This, then, is what I can do. Have done.

My gaze hard on his face. I feel ruthless, a hard core of anger building.

He takes a step back.

and last

A rapid swell chokes me.

He shakes his head, backs away, lifts his hand and brushes tears from his cheek. He reaches the door, moves through it and disappears. I hear the swing. My heart jumps then slows and the stab in my neck fades, releases my held breath.

there will never be another

*

On the third day, they wheel me to the x-ray room to take another look. Just to be sure. Dr. Powers directs them to take images of my neck straight on. He stays. There is no turning of my head.

They snap pictures.

I wait.

Later, Dr. Powers strides in and says my neck looks stable. That my vertebrae haven't re-shifted to their original positions, but that they're holding still. He tells me to wear the foam brace for one full month, then check with my doctor back home, who will need to take it from there.

Back on my feet, clutching the nurse's arm, I wobble towards the exit. Just a few dozen hours of rest and my limbs need to re-form their relationship to ground.

Mother appears, pats my hand, as the glass doors slide open to Father and family waiting at the car.

BACK TO THE SUN

Nine Mile Road—
newly-wakened grass, spruce like feather dusters, the air glassy bright and bold. You aren't expecting to find him there. You are surprised, not like you've just had a sip of coffee and realize it needs sugar but like you reach for your lover on the other side of the bed and grip only cold cotton. Somewhere else. Not there.

In a restaurant—
dark wood gleaming, empty fingerprinted glasses on the table, ashtrays heaped with cigarette butts. There, with a group of five others, one arm stretched behind the woman who would always be near and was already his wife, the other draped casually across the table, still holding a half-filled glass. The smell of smoke and liquor follows them home, floating in darkness, invisible but present. It rises silently from the laundry basket in the bedroom closet, transporting them back to that evening until the stiff smell of detergent replaces the scent of that recollection. Then it settles into the depths of memory where that smell might recall a hundred other nights that have melded into one long happening, loose and misty. You know how that goes.

At the beach—
one bare foot on hot sand, the other resting on the wind-worn
wooden seat of a picnic bench, the remains of the afternoon's lunch
still scattered across its slatted top. The sun ruffles his hair and the
breeze reflects off the water in the background. A carefully
constructed village of sand sprawls behind the table, pebbles marking
its farthest reaches, seagull feathers crowning its highest peaks, tiny
shells decorating the sides of the transitory structures his hands have
smoothed. Grains of sand are caught beneath his nails and between his
toes and, despite his best efforts, he will carry some of them home with
him where they will settle, in the bottom of the washing machine and
in between the floorboards, largely unseen but present. Two children
are still building in the sand but a third, the youngest girl, eyes large
and shy beneath her sun-hat's brim, stands in front of him: the fingers
of his left hand spread across her chest. You imagine the woman
watching him with their nieces and nephews, with the chatter of her
own childlessness in the background, not like conversation but like the
steady drone of absence. You can still feel that leg you leaned against:
sandy, warm, and solid.

On the open porch in back of the old white frame house—
a glass of something iced on the wooden railing that brackets
the door into the summer kitchen, condensation trickling down and
settling in a circle. He has one leg crossed, its ankle resting on the
opposite knee, the sole of his shoe half turned to the camera, worn
more on one side than the other. His frame casts a lean and tall
shadow on the wood warmed by sunshine, spilling over the narrow
kitchen chair. He has carried it out into the sun, where it is obvious
that it has been repainted several times, its top layer a soft shell pink in
most places. She is perched on the step, leaning sideways against the
railing, her glass resting on one knee, dampening the flimsy fabric of
her summer dress. She smiles contentedly into the space on the other
side of the photograph. His forehead is wide and smooth and his
mouth is turned up in a near-smile, not like you're midway through a

joke and realize you've heard it before but like you're watching children at play beside a field of zinnias.

Against a car—

a starry grin stretched across his face, trousers long and full, his white shirt gleaming nearly as brightly as that new chrome. You think if he'd been born fifty years later, he'd have been a model instead of a salesman in Critchley's Menswear. You think that's why she snapped thousands of pictures of him. You think you'd have fallen in love with those streamlined cheekbones too. You know she is smiling behind the camera, the sunshine aback of her dress revealing more than the modesty of that age allows, an inimitable exuberance focused on the man she loves, who rests against a machine that seems permanent and irrevocable but which only a few years later will be replaced and yield that same glossy grin.

In front of the china cabinet—

the flash in the glass doors casts shadows on dishes, figurines, and hand-painted eggs. His uniformed shoulders seem wider than the cabinet. The khakis stand, durable and stalwart, alongside her full-length gown, which shimmers not like July heat hanging over asphalt but like your eye skips across the lake when you are watching the sun set, its beauty fragmented into a million tiny shards. They are dressed for his younger sister's wedding. Her eyes are dark, her lipstick looks wet, and you know they are both breathing in the scent of vanilla she wears, warm and promising. If you concentrate, you can almost see their bodies move with that breath, elusive and artful.

Inside a department store portrait studio—

the green backdrop, meant to look leafy and lush but obviously false, outlining shoulders that are slightly rounded, not relaxed but as if they have been carrying something heavy for far too long. Her head is cocked to one side as though straining to hear the sound of her lover's heartbeat. Her left hand rests gently on his right, the ring on her fourth finger no longer gleaming. Only one week later, with that hand that she holds, its veins skating across the thin surface of his flesh, he labels each copy of the picture "50th Anniversary" on the smooth backing, slippery and white. He writes with a black felt-tip marker, in a soft, leaning script, the tail of the 'y' smearing just a little on some of them as he slips them inside the Christmas cards she signs for the two of them. He uses the same pen to copy the addresses from the list they've used for nearly all of those years, despite all the names crossed off it now, quietly and carefully moistening the back of each stamp with the centre of his tongue.

Hillside General—

pale, green walls, thin white sheets, unintelligible murmurings from the man in the other bed, sprawled plastic tubing, drapes drawn against the too-bright sunshine. The tongue that licked the stamp on your Christmas card is now shrunken and dry. His hands, the same hands that shaped those sand castles, grip the railings of the bed and shake them, begging her to let him leave. You want to answer for her but she has told you that she still hasn't washed the clothes he was wearing eighty-four days ago when he was admitted. You know she holds them to her face when she goes home at night, praying she can fall back into time before she returns them gently to the laundry basket. You don't want to remember the smell in the room on the eighty-fifth day, when you realize that time will no longer be measured in years for this man but in hours, though you know by the effort required to draw each breath that every hour pulls at him like a year. You don't want to think that this is the image that will be remembered most clearly. You want to spread the fingers of your hands across his chest, draw the struggle there into you and forget.

With his back to the sun—

barefoot in the garden, his pants rolled up nearly to his knees, his toes curled in the rich, black earth. He is laughing, not the sort of laugh that is tied to a single humorous moment but a lasting amusement which suggests that every bit mattered. You have this one in your pocket when you ask at the gate for directions, the palm of your hand resting against it, sticky and close. You draw it out as you walk down the gravel road, holding it tightly between your thumb and forefinger, feeling the light breeze dance across it and the dampness of uncertainty in your palm.

Half kneeling—

you hold it in front of you, like an offering, the bunch of baby's breath forgotten at your side, the impossibility of finding him there glaring in black and white. Tentatively, you reach to trace the etched letters of his name, a shadow cast by your hand across the stone. Your knees skirt the edge of the rectangle of carefully raked dirt. It's not like you thought but so fresh, so rich, so alive.

she walks for days
inside a thousand eyes
(a two-spirit story)

**on the other side are the correlatives for a balanced life: education,
process & ceremony**

**as sure as the moon is round
a rose is a rose is a red red rose**

rosehip and raspberry tea
holding hope like a fresh water bloom
close to the edge and very green

these are my thoughts, random and soft, as the evening sun shifts
under a bluebacked sky. off to the west I see a flock of crows pestering
a small spotted eagle, and being they all appear to be heading straight
for this grandmother tree, I'm face to face with my personal power as
a two-spirit woman. I see a drawing that took painstaking generations
to complete, all clouded and shrouded and scribbled-over, carefully,
methodically, and smudged with the palm of a hand, my own hand. I
know the drawing is the love I found inside me when I was born.
there, I see the face of my baby granddaughter, my son's small gray
hairs, my daughter's long expressive fingers and hands, the way she
moves the hair from her face in a brush stroke, a painting waiting to
be put to canvas. I see my partner, sitting with her back to a tree,
raining warm meadows of life worth every moment in time.
then I'm seeing out from the underside of the sand, from
inside the sand, upward, through fresh water green. sand pulls myself

under, holds me warm and cleans even the most intense stain. the sun and earth are my mothers, the moon my grandmother, and I see the small spotted eagle look down at me from her mother's grandmother's nest, a young crow clinging to her back.

she reaches down
and takes my hands
pulls me to a stand
her hands a life her touch
the sea

and me
bewildered
to lose the way or road
to choose
a thought
a word
a shame a doubt
a whisper on the breeze
you can't go half way on this road
and then stop there

and so begins my fast. well into the night I build the lodge the way I'm taught. I gather the grandmothers and grandfathers the way I'm taught and build a fire, and just as the sun is rising, just as I see the small spotted eagle and the young crow circle overhead, I feel the presence of many women and I prepare to enter the lodge.

beverly little thunder
standing rock lakota woman
I attended the sweat lodge ceremonies
aware
of my responsibility

to teach my children
to guide them
in the ways of their ancestors

now
to hold wimmin-only sun dances
each full moon of july
in the hills of california
two-spirit womyn
prepare
and honor
the sun dance

connie fife
cree woman
i write who i am
from my perspective
as well as from the place
most people would like me to stay

ink flows to paper slowly

for as an indian lesbian
living in a racist
homophobic society
there will always be people
who wish to keep me
silenced

so
when i am quiet

beth brant
bay of quinte mohawk woman
I find this kind of generosity
so indian
in its simplicity
and affirmation

beginning a new tradition
while following the edicts
of older traditions
for what we do
we do
for generations to come

we write
for ourselves
for our communities
for our people
for the young ones who are
looking
for the gay and lesbian path

for our elders who are
shamed or
sometimes painfully
mythologized
for the rocks and trees
for the wingeds and four-leggeds
and the animals who swim
for the warriors and resisters
who kept the faith
for creator
for our mothers fathers
grandmothers and grandfathers
who gave us our indian blood

it is not because
i am
allowing myself
to be further victimized
but rather i
too
await
my own eruptions

and the belief system
that courses through that blood

marjorie beaucage
metis woman
well
I think a good storyteller
takes a story
puts it out
in a community context
and leaves room

for the other persons
to tell their own stories
whether it's the viewer
or someone listening

so
while you are watching
or listening
you make your own story
in your head

I feel very certain after the lodge, reborn and a gift of knowing beyond
words. cleansed and how to create with the love for life and loss fresh
as the first crocus? tuba rose, the smell of love of life inside life. the
miracle of sweat lodge. keeps the checks in balance. body, mind, heart,
spirit and love's shadows even the smallest gesture.

**people who judge are both caught in fear
and do not know who they are**

there's this certain crow, a game-boy rider he calls himself. small spotted eagle sees him tailing among the others, and before she knows it he's on her back, literally, holding on for his life. turns out he's afraid of heights, though he only admits this in so many words. what he says is, crow at one time was pure white, with the sweetest singing voice of all the birds. like many others, he volunteers to steal fire from the people who live east of grandmother moon, but, being a perfectionist, he takes so long hovering over the fire—trying to find the perfect piece to steal—his white feathers smoke to black. when he returns to his village he tries to sing the first rap tune, but he's inhaled so much smoke that out comes a raw, kaw, kaw, and his flight pattern's been off ever since.

now this in-crowd crow says a basket was left at the side of the road for the woman, and since he gave his maw-caws his word in return for breakfast in bed all next week, he'd like to keep his distance. she'll need what's in there, thinks the crow, so small spotted eagle agrees to set down the basket next to the lodge. she's here to gift a story, that small spotted eagle tells him, and she asks this crazy crow could he unhook himself from her back now and leave her feathers he's toe-combed from her back, leave them in the basket for the woman, she'll need those too and stay and play awhile away, hey?, and so goes this story.

it is said that once
long time ago
two extraordinary young women
after dreams of future days
of prayer songs
of medicine ways
and loving only women
refuse marriage
to any man

after many years
while still young
the two women meet and grow
in power
in strength
in love

while most young men
respect the gifted ones
who see as true women
who see as true men
there are two young men who
fancy themselves to be
alluring appealing charming
tempting interesting fascinating
attracting captivating
beyond splendor
and follow the women
in secret

so that even after the elders tell them
no
let these women be
the men persist
and in time are forbidden
even
to speak
to be
in their company

then one fine summer day
all hush and hush
far into the woods
where the women peel
and collect tree bark

and bathe themselves nearby
the men follow

in the water the women
express their love
their passions sweet
and the men are witness to this
moment movement mystery time
when one of the women
the older one

transforms but half her beauty
into the needle of a pine
and that half
floats on the water
to the mouth of her companion
the younger one
who swallows
and soon after becomes
big with child
a green-eyed child whose name
soft-shell turtle woman
remains in song

and so it is said
that from the water
they obtained
their spirit power

and so it is said too that not too long ago, when the forests are still
strong, city doctors kill a medicine woman, calling her a witch,
because they are in a jealous rage after she heals a woman they aren't
able to heal. she is so powerful, she uses only water, bathes and prays
for the woman for four days and brings her back to full health. this is
how this story is told to small spotted eagle by her grandmother, who

is told by her grandmother, who is told by her grandmother is how small spotted eagle is told in her language.

neither the fire flared up into her friend the air
nor have the leaves begun to yellow

letter to mimshakwa:

   I'm happy to say I'm feeling much better today, and I have lots I want to say. first off, it's very cold outside and it snowed, even though there's still a fly in the fourth chamber and a couple of days ago a spider lowers in front of me from a thick evergreen, in the dark. I sense her presence and there she is, eye-level. she asks me, am I an artist and she says, you are very beautiful, both inside and out and you have very intelligent eyes. it's only one person in a hundred looks as you do.

   so today I look inside, eyes closed for a moment, and I ask myself, what's there? some pain, and then, there we are me and you, feeling for something to hold on to. something out on the water, and we're floating on top of a wooden raft, wet, warm, free, happy. we keep jumping into the water, warm and ready for the sound, that pulling sound from around the water sound, a sound that doesn't happen anywhere else. the water's warm and calls out your name to come here and feel how much we have together, our bond fluid and now to go underearth, like in my chambers, looking for what that's for, that water under mother, and we see grandmother gopher opening her lodge so's we can stay the ring and sing.

   and then just me, myself, sitting, hands over face, crying my tears into my open palms, hiding there my own salt and water, longing for happiness, poppy seed cake and baby steps under a full moon sky opening her heart to my need for water balance throughout my body.

   so, after all that, I'm feeling so much better I decide to check my email, and here I have a message marked urgent that's dated weeks ago, from a professor wisecrow, senior vice president,

otherworldly affairs. he asks me to leave a basket for you at the side of
the road where you and your car went missing, that you'll need the
four sacred medicines and I'm to include a letter, to write a poem to
proclaim the sacred medicines, and then I'm to pin a note to the basket
that says,

my girl,
if you get tired from flying
you can throw down the stone to land on

like a tiny seed
a sage seed
a whole world of view
to find her way
home
to her mother
to grow
surrounded by all her big sisters
and much older relatives

especially when a girl comes by
or a boy or woman or man
but especially a girl
who takes the time to stop
and talk
or sing too
and pick some sage for medicine
picks in a good way
prays to the four directions and offers tobacco

offers tobacco to her little sisters
the sage
and thanks her for giving up her life
to help others
to benefit from the smoke of this medicine

taking her prayers to the great spirit
purifying her in body
mind heart spirit

becoming a sister to that sage
a life-long family bond
the quiet
the peace brought to that girl who picks
medicine given freely
by the spirit of that sage
        just to walk among the sage brings awe and healing. it is said
if you wear sage leaves in your shoes you will walk goodness into
every move of your day and you can keep some in your pocket to
protect you from any and all manner of negativity. sage is the woman's
medicine and we can bless ourselves, cleanse ourselves with her
incense. sage is the closest to my heart and sweetgrass is the closest to
my spirit. sweetgrass is like an all-knowing doctor, a woman of all
ages with the attributes of a sacred, to be treated very special, to be
treated with the gift of a seer, who witnesses our deepest fears and joys
and holds them for us to see like precious gems. cedar is from the deep
—the deep, deep places of mystery in our lives and can bring clarity to
a puzzling behaviour at unexpected times. these medicines hold
knowledge in its purest and uncensored form and, like tobacco,
deliver thought, prayer, directly to the great spirit.

sweet dreams mimshakwa
and may your most tender parts
rest
on the back
of a buffalo
whose strength
whose wisdom
whose courage
will walk you into the blizzard
face first and to the place

that green green place
before the storm

love's tender tears
gopher (with one eff)

p.s. I'm home   smudged   and ready for love

either the promise of wisdom's breath
or barely audible yet distinctly red

water and wind and fine
fine breath of afternoons and reading all day long
a door
like the water
waves that pool ahead
in the heat on the highway
floors and doors and open spaces

voice full
and free to cocoon
the soothe
of mother's breath
a giving of permission
her spirit self and tenderness beyond her softest
peaceful dreams

sweet dreams womb spirit lingers
a knowing   named
so much going on and wind
all around
the cloth on the basket
dances to the sweet   the smell
burns a prayer

a love for children   candle
newly born   of thought
straddles the other side of sight
a touch

I am earth   mother   I nurture with care and grace
my children   darkness and light   death and renewal
trust   as the seed of the newly formed   I am all that you need and
I give all that I am   and yet so much destruction in so
short a time   ask the cockroach ask the loon   the
ancient bones of your ancestors   digging for gold oil bleeds the
land   earthquake
tremor sale

                    bye now

**not only are they blueblack from rump to crown
but also each feather of a crow is brown**

          well if a title like that doesn't just spoil the whole effect. like
the dream I have the other morning. I'm on a horse, tan brown and
spotted, with a loose, long mane, a twin who was birthed with special
knowledge. she's taking me to the airport and she says she thinks I'm
the most grounded person she's ever met, that I do a lot for people and
my memory is biased. the whole time there's this little bird in my
pocket. well, well, says the little bird, now this is living, and off she
goes to the mountains to have a new life. the dream goes on so long I
stop off at the side of the road to get some cat kibbles and bottled
water.
          truth is, I have a thing for cat kibbles and bottled water that
goes beyond the grave and back to the nest. an acquired taste, says
maw-caw. she tells me this story, maw-caw. she tells me long time ago
she sees this woman walking along with a young boy, a city boy. he's
happy, you can tell, and he feels real safe with this woman in her

ribbon shirt and cut off jeans. so along walks that woman in her
ribbon shirt and that boy and down on the sidewalk, hopping, kind of
scared-like, looking, crouching, limping, there's a baby crow. that
woman in her ribbon shirt says to the boy, she says, my boy, I think
that baby crow needs help. what do you think?, and the boy stops to
look with the woman in her ribbon shirt, who leans down close and
sits on the sidewalk in her cut off jeans and talks real soft to that baby
crow, says you look hurt little baby, little friend, can you come with
me for help? there's a vet just half a block away and we can take you
there, and her gentle hold lifts the baby crow up to her warm.

in the vet's office that vet person says to that woman in her
ribbon shirt and cut off jeans, you can't bring that bird in here, lady. that's
a wild bird you've got there. we don't treat wild animals here. the woman
in her ribbon shirt looks at the baby bird and she says to that baby bird,
you hear that, my child? they're calling you a wild animal and here you
live in the city just like the rest of us, isn't it? we'll cover your ears so's you
don't have to hear this kind of talk. the vet person tells her, we can give
you a wooden box for the bird or you can leave it here and we'll put it
down. the bird won't feel anything, lady. you can come in while we do it if
you prefer. the kid can come too.

we just want to know what's wrong with the little bird is all,
says the woman in her ribbon shirt. she seems injured and hungry and
thirsty. she's small, as you can see, a baby still, and her eyes are cloudy
with confusion. the vet person sighs real loud, ho-hums, ho-hums,
says, take her away in this box, then, lady, and help her yourself if you
think you can. she looks close to death anyway, the vet person says. it
probably has bugs, you know, and how do you know it's a she?

the woman in her ribbon shirt stands there a few minutes,
thinking, and the boy starts to cry softly, his ice cream dripping bubble
gum smells on the outside of the wooden box and onto the floor. the
woman in her ribbon shirt stands there a while longer and helps the
boy feel better, tells him they will take this little urban crow with them
and help whatever way they know how. she asks do the vet people
have a bit of cat food and water to spare, and they say, no, we're
closing. take the wild bird and leave, lady. there's no telling what

kinds of bugs and diseases that bird has brought into our waiting area and we have sick animals in the back. so, if you don't mind, lady?, please leave the office.

so out they walk and the woman in her ribbon shirt talks real gentle to that baby crow, real slow and sing-song-like as she walks over to the gayway store to buy some cat kibbles, bottled water, and a soft travel pillow. well now—maw-caw always says that when she's winding down—well now, that young crow eats some of the little brown kibbles, drinks some bottled water and falls fast asleep in that wooden box. wakes up couple hours later in the river, with the woman in her ribbon shirt washing him with the speed of an uphill leak, feather by feather.

turns out that baby crow was all tree-sapped, all stuck together like middle-of-the-road road-kill giblets on a crowded summer highway. would've died that day, that baby crow, says maw-caw. well now, wouldn't you know it?, that baby crow was me, though I have to say I don't remember a darn thing except I'm sap-shy and I like my water bottled to this day.

maw-caw tells me it's cuz of what that woman in her ribbon shirt does for me that day in the river, the same woman over there who's building a sweat lodge?, that's why I get along so good with the women, and that's why, like the women, I have the gift with the water. that one I didn't know myself until this one day I hear my relative talk about that over at the indian friendship centre downtown over by the river. I'm playing the piano at the time and that's how I remember her words that day.

sylvia maracle
bay of quinte mohawk woman
the thing that strikes me about the water
is the water
will take the shape
of its vessel
a ceremony bowl

whether rock or pottery
wood or copper

water
strongest force on the earth
even wind can't do
what water can do
to determine
the process of life

and we know
water comes first
before life itself
we know
water has responsibilities
to cleanse us
to quench us
to nourish our thirst
to allow us to sit beside it
to find peace

whether a single drop
or the largest body
water represents
the female element
our role
our capacity
to take to make
those shapes

as women
we have
the power of the water
of every day
to change the shape of the thing

SELAH

2.

Morning sun snatched away three times
: conflict's dragon folds and wrestles cloud

dirtied in foreign conflict. Below-
red soil rich in calcium. Discipline

propagates moral courage, cinching
wisdom's waist: a girl in her five years and

her swirly circle of red and white striped poplin.
Higher intelligence flows into the next discipline.

3.

Wild fire's form is result and attribute of its rage and controversy.
Take my brother, for instance. He has begun many times and finishes
quivering at the mid-point of the mountain, its stillness and
stubbornness unmoved by blazes. He dared not decide on grace and
beauty even though he had laid aside his garments and proceeded in
his nakedness, his freckled beauty astonishing to the alpine flowered
meadows, to himself even. He is nearly purified. He walks into the
unmingled house, a hut really, where he knows the God who sits
behind an army surplus metal desk, smokes a cigar and asks of him to
prove the worth of his existence by what beauty he has produced. My
brother offers his two children, golden curly-haired cherubs in the
ninety-ninth percentile for weight, a staircase that fell beautifully and
another that failed him as he attempted its repair, his descent on it
unglorious and injurious. God hrumphs in his usual way. My brother
is confused, turns his day so the front is at the back, like a T-shirt with
stains hidden by the protection of a jacket, always necessary in the rain
forest. His descent meets with the Apart, the Pure, the Existence who
see his beginning and his end and excuse this middle.

4.

Beauty's love demands beauty's gladness as it falls like a shaft of wheatstraw bright as sun on January snow. Patience bides its molten time. It waits for rain, the abysmal floods hunger for veritable heaven: a wooden house small under elms.

5.
A light blue cotton dress, a string of Japanese pearls
: the comeliest of daughters welcomes

her husband walking toward her on board
a train, dust motes rising into air.

8.
Joyful threesies, last night thunder
blocked the highway, crows evicted from their nests
travel impeded to the east. Adversity darkens mass
deflected by light behind veils. A father behind a veil
but there it is: a mother unresistingly yields.

12.
You weren't flying yesterday, were you, my brother? Someone has been terrorizing. It is time to avoid. There are terrorized people everywhen. Hatred is white ash rising over human endeavour as it crashes in flames, clinging to babies swimming at the Y, daddies at work, mothers sorting laundry, stock brokers getting coffee, Palestinian kids starving, Rwandan kids orphaned, Cree kids sniffing gasoline. It splits apart: the roof will collapse: it has weakened: don't go anywhere.

13.
Dwelling as if in consecrated precincts, even common ways
profane deliverance from the rain. Pressure released-

yellow brightens the day, an arrow to shoot at thought, pierces
thunder, splits sound from beauty, two halves of perseverance:

choose friends wisely, Plotinus would tell you. Porphyry, a student,
became a friend, unscrambled his thought in Greek: gratitude for
deliverance.

14.
And so measurelessness against measure, the evil
act can come out of nowhere, comes from
behind in its absence of goodness, pushes
nestlings into hostile air as into a vacuum.

Thunder seems closer in the mountains.

15.
All alone on the dangerous journey
one pushes ego down into the valley

which fills with waters of blushing modesty
water rises, mountain crumbles, accomplishment.

Real is the strength to push across currents
which zip underfoot

stones slippery concentration
matter wraps like a fog

to confuse thought but
merit causes greater bewilderment.

16.
Up from the toes half-remembering heaven
the lame arm lowers its shoulder

round the hedge comes a view of the mountain
heaven, fog lifting, trees sparkle

larch copper, aspen yellow, maple red
but soul continually, repeatedly stays behind

17.

The wagoner's cart can take heavy loads because of its great axle. It rolls over roughest existence, searching its bed for resolution: cargo jumps, settles.

My dog is a china dog. He is grey and he howls mutely into desk space. My other dogs are dead of human stupidity.

The evil act comes as if out of nowhere but it is always from the same place of fecund multiplicity, Plotinus said. It is the one hand. The other hand is as invisible, untouched by evil acts: the rat that bites the baby asleep in her crib, the night bombing of a city of orphans, the early morning collusion of self-righteous hatred and commerce. They make hostages of those acting and acted upon.

In timeless flesh, the trip is arduous when one half of the body is lame. The wagoner's wagon, your body, moves slowly. It waits at the bottom of the mountain, the sliding down part, waiting for an opening. The wagoner, your mind, looks within. You are behind him wondering what the heck. His hat is pulled over his eyes. He wears red, fluffy ear mugs. He can't hear anything and it seems he likes it that way. You wait for his waiting to end. The wagoner clears the way. He is the sherpa of personal cargo, knows to wait for direction. Your lame side is less heavy as you begin again.

18.
The good is that on which all else depends, said Plotinus.

The small boy leaps into deepest waters.
Joy: *It sounds like coconuts*
down there, he says.

The young man climbs a cell phone tower
in the cold of Northern Alberta's October, wonders:
what is the good?

Take spinach for example, its puffiness
textured veins of systole: what of its good you might wonder.

Sometime you might climb a sea island's hills to find yellow dwellings,
each more marvellous than the last. The diastolic good builds. The sea
has meanwhile covered your return path, hems you there for the
night. You decide to try to return to the mainland anyway, gripping a
cable that sinks deeply into the green water and your feet no longer
touch the slippery boardwalk. You might marvel at the ascending
goodness.

And then you forget the good. It gets easier (to forget the good).

Your last journey will be in a bed, you hope
people you love will see you to the end, you will
depend upon the love they offer even though you alone
must go through the curtain past craving, past diastole into expansion.

Dreams reverse the order; leave you alone in your confusion and closure
but in bed with someone who kisses you. Such lonely privilege.

THE LIFE OF A LOSER: A WORK-IN-PROGRESS (SO TO SPEAK)

This little overview of sorts is comprised of two kinds of accounts: first-hand accounts and second-hand accounts. At the risk of sounding obvious, second-hand accounts are descriptions of my experiences as told to me by someone else, usually my mother. These are experiences I have no recollection of, but someone else, usually my mother, does. The fact that someone else remembers bits and pieces of your life that you don't is great. Except when that someone is my mother.

I say this not to be mean, but because I suspect my mother's first-hand accounts are somewhat lacking in accuracy. I can remember numerous times my mother has relayed family stories to her friends. I wouldn't have thought twice about her vivid description of this experience or that experience, except for the fact that I had been there myself. Yes, she does have a way with mangling history so it is no longer recognizable. Ketki, my big sister, will back me on this one. It was one of those frequent occurrences that was so incredibly irritating and mind-boggling, but humourous at the same time. Pointing out the inaccuracies in her stories was futile, even when you had the starring role in one of her many stories. What I still haven't figured out to this day is whether my mother was ever aware that her stories were not quite fact. Rather, they were, at best, fiction based on a true story. Unfortunately, for the early years, this is the majority of what I have to go on.

The Early Years: The Birth of a Loser

The early years started on January 6, 1969—yes, the day I was born—in Kanpur, India. Unfortunately, I don't remember too much of this experience. And I don't have any exciting birth stories to relay to you, as no one has relayed any to me.

Oh, except the one about how my head was stuck in the "birth canal" for a long time. This was told to me (many years after the fact), by my mother of course, to explain how the defect of my left eyebrow came to be. You know, the one I hadn't actually noticed until my mother pointed it out. I consciously couldn't stand just about every part of my body from a very early age, but I have to admit, I hadn't really put too much thought into my eyebrows until then. Or my big head (which later came back to haunt me). Anyway, I'm not sure if that really counts as a birth story. Especially since I don't think my defective eyebrow has much of anything to do with my birth experience. And, if it did, I can't imagine the doctors noticed, let alone pointed this out to her, at the time. Which means, yes, that she came up with this interesting theory all by herself. And, quite honestly, I'm not sure she even noticed my eyebrow at the time. And, if she did, why? Any way you look at it, I can't help but come to the conclusion that my mom is a bit of a strange cookie.

Which reminds me of another wonderful birth story told to me just over a year ago by my mother—how could I have forgotten? Characteristically written in an extremely uncharacteristic manner for her, my mother wrote the following in my birthday card for 2002: "It seems like yesterday that I was holding a bundle of joy (a second one of course) in my hands and a friend of mine said, 'Hey, you have such a beautiful baby' and how happy I felt just looking at you. Oh! Time flew so fast, but I still remember so many fond memories of the time." Whatever. This was a story she felt was so noteworthy she had to tell me it 33 years after my birth? That some friend of hers told her I was a cute baby? Now whether that was the case or not, what friend of hers wouldn't say something like that about her baby? Please. And I'm sure her friend (whose name you'll notice she doesn't seem to mention) said 'Hey'. All that being said, I don't actually believe my mom has any specific recollection of any of this occurring. Not really a birth story either.

There is only one other story I have to tell that is somewhat related to my birth, but once again, not actually a birth story. It was probably when I was about five or six years old that I first began to question whether or not my parents were in fact my "real" parents. Thanks to Danny Partridge, I began to question everything. That's right—I'm talking about the Partridge Family episode where Danny, feeling different than the rest of the Partridge clan due to his red hair and all, is convinced he was adopted. Now I didn't (and still don't) have red hair or any other such obvious, tangible difference from my family. But as a child, I definitely felt deep-down different and unloved by my parents. Not only did I feel like somebody out there could understand how I felt (even if it was Danny Partridge), but everything was starting to make sense. I don't think I was aware of the concept of adoption before seeing this life-changing episode. After it, it was all I could think about for months.

My mom spent endless hours trying to convince me that she and my dad were, in fact, my biological parents. But to me, everything she and my father did, or didn't do, was new-found proof that they didn't really love me, that they weren't actually my parents. My mother finally rummaged around and found "proof" that this was the family I was born into. The proof consisted of three photographs—two taken at exactly the same time, supposedly right after I was brought home from the hospital following my birth. My mother and my sister are sitting next to a newborn me in these photos. The other was supposedly of me as an infant, a huge 8"x 10" infant that I still think looks nothing like me. I have a feeling that my mom has no idea who the child in the picture is. Anyway, I accepted this questionable proof and finally let it go, at least on the surface.

The Silverstone Era (4-7 years)

I think it is around age four or five that my ability to recall and provide substantial quantities of first-hand accounts kicks in. Four was the age I started elementary school and the age when we moved into our first house at 610 Silverstone Avenue.

My bedroom in this new house of ours was decorated (I use that word loosely) by my parents. It had a pink frilly bedspread and drapes—so 'me', you know?—and, get this, red and black carpet. Either my parents had a mean sense of humour or bad taste. Or both. I remember Ketki's bedroom. She had a double bed with a relatively nice bedspread and drapes with large blue and purple flowers. Her carpet was also mixture of blue and purple. I swear they liked her better.

Downstairs, there was a carpeted area, with a little wet bar off to the side. The carpet was a yellowish outdoor carpet with small red and brown splotches all over it. Yes, it was as bad as it sounds. There was a couch and chair in that area. Behind the carpeted area was the play area, the "rec room", covered with brown and white linoleum. The walls were covered with fake wood panelling. The whole scene was about as tacky as it gets. Off the play area was my dad's study. An odd musty room with the thinnest dark brown outdoor carpeting, a mattress on the floor, a desk, a run-down green bathroom and an ashtray because he was relegated to this room to smoke. We also had a big backyard encompassed by a white wooden fence, interrupted only by our unattached garage. The school I went to was just down the block. Kindergarten and Grade 1 were off in a small, separate, cream-coloured school house.

I look back on the days of Silverstone and think, in some ways, I was just your average little girl. Sometimes my sister and I would play Barbies. My sister had Barbie's Dream House. As shallow as Barbie seems, apparently she didn't dream very big. Nor did she dream of furniture, other than a white plastic bed. We spent a number of hours making up various scenarios. My sister and her multiple Barbies donning multiple outfits. Me with Ken, GI Joe and Big Jim. GI Joe was a hand-me-down from some family friends who had a teenage son. Not only did I get GI Joe, but I got his Jeep, which I absolutely loved. My sister had Barbie's brightly-coloured, happy-looking camper and I had GI Joe's tough-looking Jeep. We played together, but we were kind of in different worlds.

Big Jim was a Christmas gift from my parents. One of the few I remember really wanting and really liking. You may not have heard of Big Jim before. He never did make it to the big time. He was short, muscular and—are you ready for this?—he could wield a mean karate chop. That's right—just press the button on his back to bring his arm up and down with lightning speed. He was my favourite. At some point, my sister acquired the Sunshine Family. An odd couple with a baby that rode on their canopy-covered bicycle-built-for-two. Give me a break. For a while I added Mr. Sunshine to my collection, but quickly returned him to his family. I've never been the judgmental type, but I'm sorry, Mr. Sunshine was a scrawny wimp. I had no doubt that Big Jim could karate chop him in half and I didn't want that to happen. And he was just a little too happy for my liking. It was bad enough that I allowed Headless Ken (his head didn't stay on very well, causing him to frequently self-decapitate) to join the ranks of GI Joe and Big Jim. At least Ken had the headless thing going on. He had issues. His life wasn't perfect. Big Jim, GI Joe and Headless Ken—in some ways I wasn't your average little girl.

Having few friends, I played alone much of the time. As my first grade teacher kindly pointed out on my report card: "She is very friendly and the other children respond well to her although she does not have one particular friend. She seems to prefer to be alone on many occasions." I think it was for this reason Ketki went out of her way to play with me. In addition to playing with Barbie and the crew, the two of us had a "secret club" which met once a week. We met in our "secret clubhouse", Ketki's bedroom closet. We had comforters and pillows piled on the floor and we pulled her little lamp into the closet so we could actually see each other. She was president and she graciously allowed me to be vice-president of this special club. I felt so important, never wondering why I couldn't be president. Every week she would take attendance on her little attendance sheet. I kid you not. I don't remember what pressing issues we discussed, but remember loving these top-secret meetings. She was, and still is, a great big sister.

Now, I think it was my fifth summer that I spent going to day camp. The camp itself wasn't too memorable, except for the fact that it was the site where my big head—you know, the one that was so problematic at the time of my birth—came back to haunt me. As official campsters, we were supposed to order special 'Happy Face' T-shirts to wear to camp everyday. A white T-shirt with a big, yellow happy face plastered on the front. For some reason, I thought they were the coolest thing and could not wait for them to arrive.

When the T-shirts finally arrived, I rushed to go put mine on. Much to my dismay, however, I couldn't actually get it on. Although it was the appropriate size for my body, I could not seem to get it over my head. My big, fat head. But I kept on trying, using force close to the point of ripping it, but no luck. I brought it home with me that night for an 'extended' fitting session, thinking maybe with a bit of stretching and pulling I could 'make' it fit. But my second attempt was also futile and the T-shirt had to go back.

I went back to camp the next day, hoping to hear stories from other kids who also struggled in vain to get this defective lot of T-shirts over their heads. But no such stories surfaced. All that surfaced were a bunch of happy-faced kids wearing their 'Happy Face' T-shirts. It was hard to be inconspicuous, being the only one without one. Not only did I not want to stand out, to be the different one, I also didn't really want to explain why I didn't have one. I was one unhappy camper. But, in the end, I guess I was never meant to wear a happy face. No sir, the symbolism wasn't lost on me.

The days of Silverstone also mark the beginning of my many creative failures. Grade 1 was my first foray into creative writing. I'm the first to admit my stories were less than brilliant. However, given I was just learning to write PERIOD, I think my report card assessment was pretty harsh. "I'm a little disappointed in her creative writing. I feel she could be writing longer and more interesting stories than she is." On reviewing my daily Grade 1 journal, complete with illustrations by yours truly, I'm not arguing that I was a particularly creative kid. No, if anything, this journal highlights my lack of creativity in writing and in life in general. I was, at that time, and for many years to follow, the biggest TV junkie I know.

Here, for your reading pleasure, are a few excerpts from my Grade 1 journal, original spelling mistakes included and my added comments in brackets:

Wednesday, December 1st: Yesterday we went shopping [illustration of Safeway included]. Tomorrow is a half a day and I am going to play with my friend.

Thursday, December 2nd: I am going to watch TV tomorrow [illustration of TV included]. Today am going to play school with my friend because we get a half a day.

Friday, December 3rd: Today I am going to watch TV [did I mention that already?; illustration of TV included]. On Saturday were going to someones house.

Monday, December 6th: Today I go to Brownies and we are having a Christmas party [illustration of a white, blond-haired me in my Brownie outfit included]. Everybody has to bring a gift under $1.00. Yesterday we had guests.

Tuesday, December 7th: Next week we are going to put up our Christmas tree. On Sunday I am going to two birthday partys.

Wednesday, December 8th: Yesterday I went shopping [illustration of Zeller's included].

Thursday, December 9th: Last night we went shopping at Woolco and gambles [illustration of both included; my teacher capitalized the 'g' of gambles—the only error she noted in the whole damn journal! Yikes!]

Tuesday, December 14th: Yesterday we had a Christmas concert in the afternoon and in the evening at 7:30 my mom and dad came. In the evening. I was in the choir. [yep, no grammar problems there].

Wednesday, December 15th: Tomorrow my sister has guitar lessons [I'm getting desperate here . . .]. Today we get half-a-day. On Friday I going to watch a show on TV with Jerry Lewis at 10:30.

Thursday, December 16th: Today we are going to put up are Christmas tree [yikes!]. Yesterday I was making my Christmam list. Tomorrow I am going to watch television. Last night we had Mexican food for dinner [interesting, eh?].

Tuesday, December 21st: Tomorrow my sister is going to ballet [desperation rearing its ugly head again]. Today I am going to watch the nutcracker.

You get the idea . . . I don't think anyone can argue with the fact that this is boring, uninspired writing reflecting a boring and uninspired life. But it probably would be a bit more helpful for someone—say, a teacher or a parent—to sit down and help me write and live a little more creatively. We're talking about a five year old, for crying out loud.

And then one day, I turned six. Still sorely lacking in creativity, might I add. It was my dream at that time to be a firefighter or a garbage collector when I grew up. I'm not sure my dream had much more thought put into it than wanting a job where I could ride in a big truck. Fire engine. Garbage truck. It didn't really matter, as long as it was big and a truck. So when my mom asked me what I wanted for my birthday cake that year, I let her know that I was debating between a fire engine and a garbage truck. I was the only one debating this question. A fire engine it was. In retrospect, I'm kind of surprised my parents went along with the fire engine cake and didn't force me to have a ballerina cake, a princess cake or just a plain old cake, not trying to be anything but a circle or a rectangle.

However, my birthday presents were a different story. I think most of them were an attempt on my parents' part to 'convert' me into, you know, a real girl. Hence, 'Malibu Barbie' and 'Bizzie Lizzie' contaminated my birthday stash that year. You heard me—'Bizzie Lizzie'. Battery-operated 'Bizzie' wasn't just any doll. No, she came equipped with her very own iron, duster and other household appliances so she could do what she loved best—household chores. What a fun doll. Did the makers of this winner expect little girls around the world to shout out 'Look mom, look how fun it is to clean!'? Not only did I have zero interest in her, she actually kind of scared me. She was immense (I think she was about the size of a four year-old child) and she always struck me as a bit evil. But now I wish I had kept her so she could clean my apartment. I'm not sure whatever became of 'Malibu Barbie'. I don't think she even made it out of the box she came in, let alone to Malibu.

No, I wasn't too thrilled with my birthday stash that year. Not only did I not want any of it, it was far from the one thing I wanted that year and every year of my childhood I can remember—a dog. Well, actually a dog or a monkey, but I figured the odds of the monkey idea panning out were pretty slim, so I never mentioned it to anyone. I pleaded with my parents every birthday, every Christmas and pretty much every day in-between to get me a dog. That's all I would ever ask for I promised them—that would cover all my birthdays and every Christmas from then on in. I really meant it and I do believe, to this day, that I would have stuck to my promise.

But, despite my pleading, I never got a dog. Why? Well, I'm not totally sure, as my mother's reasons varied depending on what day of the week it was. On Mondays, it seemed to be related to my sister's deep-seated fear of dogs stemming back to an early childhood in India which, apparently, was filled with hoards of mangy neighbourhood stray dogs. On Tuesdays, there were concerns that I would not be responsible enough to look after a dog and the onus would end up on my parents. On Wednesdays, my mom didn't want me to have a dog because, well, she just didn't like dogs. On Thursdays, my mom brought up my dad's supposed allergy to dogs—you know, the one no one had ever mentioned before. On Fridays, I just wasn't allowed to have a dog. Why? Because my mom said so. End of discussion. You may think I'm joking, but my mom actually did use all these reasons.

I was desperate to have a dog. I needed another friend. A friend to come home to and play with, to laugh with, to cry with. Yeah, to cry with. A friend who wouldn't judge me and who would love me no matter what, a friend who would always be there and in whose eyes I wouldn't ever be a loser. Yes, I was in need of a dog. And I really do believe I would have taken excellent care of my best friend if I had been given the opportunity. But I never was.

The closest I came was when I was in Grade 1. Our class had just recently acquired Gerbil, a pet gerbil that sat in a cage on the windowsill in our classroom. One morning, shortly before Spring Break, Ms. Lechner announced that she needed somebody to take Gerbil home and look after him over the break. I couldn't believe it. This was my lucky day! This was perfect, I thought. I don't know *why*—it was only for a week and it was a *gerbil*—but it was perfect. You can't say I wasn't willing to compromise.

Ms. Lechner told us to come see her after class if we were interested in bringing Gerbil home. My heart was racing and I was dizzy with excitement. How was I supposed to concentrate for the rest of the morning? My mind was full of Gerbil-related thoughts. Would I be able to beat the mad rush at the end of class to stake my claim on Gerbil? Please God, please let me make it to Ms. Lechner's desk first. I'm not sure why I was praying—this was the same God I asked to please, please let me get a dog for my birthday. But I kept on praying and thinking and strategizing. And then, when the bell rang, I put my plan into action and was the first one to the front. Breathless, I told Ms. Lechner I wanted more than anything to bring Gerbil home for Spring Break and to please, please sign me up right away. Unlike the other times I had asked God to please, please do anything for me, it actually worked with Ms. Lechner. Gerbil would be spending Spring Break with me. This really was my lucky day. The only one I had had so far.

Ecstatic, I raced home with a big grin on my face. I told my mom about this amazing opportunity that just couldn't be passed up, not telling her that I had already signed myself up. No, no—I must create the illusion that I asked her first and that she gave me permission to bring Gerbil home. It was the perfect plan. "No," she said "you can't bring a gerbil home." *What!!?* Her words were ringing in my ears. What was I going to do? I had already committed to it. "Why not?" I inquired, no really valid reason coming to my mind. I mean, Ketki didn't spend her early childhood in gerbil-infested slums, the responsibilities involved in looking after a gerbil would be minimal, my mom had never said anything about not liking gerbils before, my dad wasn't allergic to them—I mean, what reason could there possibly be to say no? "Because I say so." Oh yeah, I forgot about that one.

I persisted over the years. Every birthday, every Christmas, I never stopped asking for a dog. Never. But I also made sure that my parents knew I would be happy with a cat, a bird, a gerbil, a fish…whatever, just as long as it wasn't human. I could make it work if I was given the chance. But I never was.

The Colorado Years: The Start of a Breakdown (24-29 years)

It was during the last two years of my five year stint in Colorado that I experienced my first breakdown. It's kind of scary when you actually have to start numbering them.

It was in February 1998 that I first contemplated seeing a therapist. At that time, I got the name and number of a therapist recommended by a friend. However, it wasn't until June of that year that I actually decided to make an appointment. By July I had already moved on to a different therapist. And by August I was somewhere I never would have guessed at the beginning of that crazy year.

There I was, waiting on a stretcher in the Emergency Department with my friend and co-worker Anne, who also happens to be a therapist. She was the one who brought me here, against my will might I add. I think it was something I said about being at peace with the idea of death that prompted her to bring me to this place. Now I remember why I don't share things with other people. Let me tell you, time does NOT fly when you are NOT having fun. I could feel every minute of those nine hours we waited until someone actually came to talk to me.

"I hope that's not who's going to be interviewing me," I say to Anne, referring to the scary-looking woman heading in our direction. "Seema?" says the scary-looking woman. My luck, of course. She is heavily, and I mean heavily, made up. In addition to her make-up, she has a look that is both severe and condescending plastered on her face.

Her stare tells me at once that she already doesn't like me one little bit. I don't know if it's the colour of my skin, the fact that I look like a dyke or the way I am dressed—or perhaps a bit of all three. I don the apparel of the depressed—an old pair of sweat pants and a ripped, paint-stained T-shirt. After totally cutting me down with one stare, she glances over at Anne, who also looks the part of a dyke, and then back at me. What she is thinking is more than a little transparent.

She then motions for us to follow her into a room with a closed door. She is accompanied by a young-looking woman, whom I presume is a student. However, she never does actually introduce herself or the young woman before beginning her barrage of questions. She begins with a few basic demographic-type questions. In response to her questions, I tell her that I grew up in Winnipeg, I have lived in Denver for three years, I went to medical school and I am currently working with the Colorado Coalition Against Sexual Assault. She then asks Anne who she is and, repeatedly, what her relationship to me is. As if she knows we are more than 'friends' and 'coworkers'—which, by the way, we are not. Anne then throws in the fact that she is a therapist. The scary-looking woman (SLW, for short) then repeatedly asks me if I am comfortable having Anne present for the interview. I assure her I am. I think the more accurate question is whether she is comfortable having Anne in the room.

Now, I don't know if I've mentioned this before, but I don't actually know why I fell apart that year. There were a number of things that happened during the preceding couple of years, but not one obvious thing that I identified as *the* cause. This is what I tell the SLW when she asks me why I fell into this deep, dark depression. And I tell her that things just got progressively worse, spiralling out of control. That I went from this incredible emotional volatility to a complete numbness I had never experienced before. At peace with death, I experienced a suicidality (yes, I know suicidality is not actually a word, yet it's the only word that seems to fit) I had never felt before. I tell her all of this to try and explain what was still unexplainable to even myself.

"So, you still haven't told me why you're so upset," the SLW says in response. *Huh?* Okay, does this woman know what depression is? I tell her I can't explain it any better than I just did and then go on to repeat what I already told her. "I still don't understand why you're so upset," she says. Being at a complete loss, I helplessly look over at Anne and she, thankfully, jumps in. "Look, I've known her for a long time and this is very different for her. There was a sudden and dramatic change that was evident when her depression began," Anne spouts. The SLW finally lets it go, although I get the sense that she feels her question remains unanswered.

We then move on to my education and career. No, I have no idea why. "You mentioned before that you went to medical school. What happened?" she asks, probing for something, I assume. "Nothing happened," I reply. "Then why didn't you finish?" "I did finish," I reply, strongly sensing that she doubts, for some appearance-based reason, that I am capable of this. "Then what?" she asks. "Then I did a one-year internship." "What happened with that?" "Nothing happened with that." "Why didn't you finish?" she repeats. This is getting more than a little tiring. "I did finish," I reply. "Then what did you do?" "Then I did a residency in Preventive Medicine." "Why didn't you finish that?" Is she for real? "I did finish." "Then why aren't you practicing medicine?" she asks, assuming that my job at the sexual assault coalition does not fall into the realm of 'medicine'. Should I tell her that I am actually practicing medicine and that I don't need a fucking career counsellor? And that her questions are so irrelevant that I want to scream? And that we're in the fucking Emergency Department, for Christ's sake? All I end up doing is spitting out an explanation of how I view my job as practicing medicine, albeit in a non-traditional way. She finally lets it go.

She then tries to assess my social support system. Being depressed and suicidal, this at least makes some sense to me. "So, do you live with anybody?" she asks. "No," I reply. "Are you in a relationship?" "Uh, no," I reply. "Do you have any friends?" I am not joking. This is what she asks me. "No, I'm a big fucking loser," I say. Well, actually, I say "You may not have noticed, but there's one sitting right beside me." Better than "Yes" but not quite as good as "No, I'm a big fucking loser" or "No, and I'm guessing you don't either." I didn't think it was possible, but she then gives me a look that is even more condescending than the one she has had on since coming across my sorry presence. I consider explaining to her that her job is to assess for depression, not induce it.

After, oh, about forty-five minutes, she decides to broach the subject of suicide. You know, the reason I am at the Emergency Department. After confirming that I am indeed suicidal, she asks me if I have a plan. "Yes," I reply. "Well, what is it?" she asks, exasperated with me yet again. "Slitting my wrists," I say matter-of-factly. "Have you made any plans, any arrangements?" she asks. "Yes," I say. "Like what?" she asks. "I've figured out what I'm going to do with my possessions. I'm going to give them to those people who are and who have been significant in my life. I've chosen possessions for each person representing my relationship with them, possessions that have some symbolic value," I say, thinking how beautiful a sentiment that is. "What else?" she hurls at me, without missing a beat. "My cats. I've figured out what I'm going to do to make sure my cats are well taken care of." "What else?" "My money. I've figured out what I'm going to do with my savings." "What else?" yet again spews from her mouth. This line of questioning is also getting more than a little bit tiring. "Letters. I want to write letters to all the people in my life who have been significant. Even if things have changed over time. I want them to know how they impacted my life in a positive way and thank them for what they've done for me," I say, once again moving my own self with the beauty of the sentiment. "What else?" She really is for real. I turn to Anne, feeling helpless once again. "Nothing else. That's it," I reply. "Hmmmm," she says knowingly. I have no idea what that's supposed to mean. I suspect she has no idea either. But then, I suspect there's very little she knows.

An hour—that's right, an hour—into the interview, Anne interrupts, having to leave for an appointment with a client. "Can you tell me what you are planning to do with her? Are you planning to admit her?" Anne asks. "I don't know yet. I have to finish my assessment." She's serious too. "Well, I'm her ride home and I would like to put my two cents in," Anne says. "I'm going to be away for the weekend and I won't be accessible. I really don't think she's safe to go home and be alone in her apartment." The SLW does her the favour of acknowledging her thoughts and says she'll take them into consideration. Anne looks at me sympathetically, mouths "I'm sorry", rolls her eyes and then exits. This at least makes me feel somewhat better.

In the meantime, I face the barrage of questions on my own. The SLW gets a kind of evil look in her eyes now that Anne is gone. "So tell me about your childhood," she continues. You have got to be fucking kidding me. "That's kind of a broad question," I say. "What exactly do you want to know?" "What is your relationship with your parents like?" she asks. I contemplate the relevance of her question and decide there is none. But, of course, I answer anyway. "Kind of detached, distant," I respond. "Any siblings?" "Yeah, one sister," I reply. "What was her relationship with your parents like growing up?" *Huh?* "Well," I begin, "I always felt like my parents favoured her because she was the perfect daughter and I was" . . . "the boy" I hear the SLW say, as she cuts me off and finishes my sentence for me. *Aha! My suspicions confirmed.* "Fuck you, you racist, homophobic bitch," I spew. Well, actually, I glare at her with a look I like to think says "fuck you", ignore her comment and finish the sentence the way I meant to . . . "not exactly what they were looking for." She looks at me, nodding her head, like this is obvious. That I wouldn't be what any parent was looking for.

Things continue for a little longer and then, finally, she decides she has enough information to decide if I should be admitted. I decide she has enough information to write my biography. Turns out I'm unsafe enough to be admitted. Up on the ward, I receive a phone call from Anne. "I am so sorry you had to endure that," she says. "If I wasn't depressed when you brought me here, I sure as hell am now. That scary-looking woman reminded me about a few depressing things about my life that I completely forgot about," I say, feeling angry and sad at the same time. "She did not like you," Anne says. Now, normally I would find this a hurtful, insulting thing for someone to point out. But at the moment, I am so happy to hear these words come out of her mouth. I need someone to validate that whole experience, validate that I am not just being oversensitive. "She wasn't too crazy about you either," I reply, referring to the whole therapist, lesbian thing.

I wake up the next morning a bit disoriented. More so than usual. I kind of feel like I don't belong here. Like I'm different than everybody else. Like I'm not really mentally ill, just sad. Really sad. But I'm sure that's what everybody else here thinks. That they're the 'normal' one, misunderstood and misplaced. I know I haven't been here long, but I can't say I like it here. For one thing, the staff want you to go to 'group' at least twice a day.

I was hesitant about the whole group thing right from the get-go. I hate to be judgmental (well, actually I like to be judgmental, I just hate that I am), but it's a little hard for me to believe that the young, perky woman leading the group can even *spell* the word 'suffer.' She solicits ideas on what those of us in the group do to make ourselves feel better when we are depressed. I want to say that I avoid locking myself up in a building with a bunch of people who are depressed . . . it just doesn't do anything for my mood.

The best suggestion is thrown out by an elderly man, who I get the feeling has been here a while. Apparently, brushing his teeth helps him escape the depths of depression. This makes me wonder about his dental hygiene when he isn't depressed. Our group leader has some additional words of wisdom. When *she's* feeling really down, she not only brushes her teeth, but brushes her *tongue* as well. I begin to wonder about her dental hygiene too. I want to go check on the door and see if I'm in the right place or if this is a seminar on 'The Dental Origins of Depression' or something.

But, I guess this is the kind of help we're supposed to get from group. Like we should all go brush our teeth and maybe, just maybe, that will get us out of this joint. I want to refute their theory, to tell them that I actually brush my teeth, and even my tongue, *every day* . . . more than once even . . . and I *still* ended up in here. I want to tell them that I think the real key may be flossing. Because, although I tell people I do, I don't actually floss *every day*. I sit there, contemplate banging my head against the wall, but decide that may work against me getting out of this place sooner than later. So, you see, it was after this experience that I decided to be the rebel patient and stay in my room instead of going to group.

present imperfect

powell street

biking down the august streets of vancouver i find my pride at powell
street. reverberating into the crowd as exuberant taiko. walk into a
sea of issei, nisei, sansei pride, generations of pride playing in rock
bands, doing park clean-up, serving corn on the cob, making videos,
doing a post-atomic dance. loud, juicy watermelon smashed open
pride. lazy summer sweet, sweaty orange pride that turns your quick
stride into a languid prowl. an icy lemon kakikori pride, melting on
my thirsty tongue. once found pride somewhere on the curve of her
nape, on the pout of her lips, in the welcome between her thighs. now
i rummage through the ashes looking for stubborn, black swishy
strands of girl pride recently shaved off. a bare nun pride. a coldblue
tightlip heartbruised pride that holds your shoulders rigid, your back
sad. pride on Salish land. kaslo, slocan, new denver, greenwood,
black & white archived internment survival pride. ragged ass bi any
means necessary random trigonometries of pride. oppenheimer park
downtown eastside strung out on the street scowling pride.
oxymoronic cop in a uniform pride. not just the usual suspects, the
flashy buffed fag dancing on a float or glittery drag queen strutting
pride but a burnaby correctional centre prisoner pride, a mom and dad
marching in pflag pride, an every day in high school pride, elementary
pride, endless legal battles to win pride, child-friendly pride, a jenny
shimizu is everywhere hello kitty hello pussy pride. kiss me like you
mean it pride. finally coming out to your momma pride that is
actually relief. scavenging alleys for art materials pride. creating our
own rituals because we need to pride. give me graffiti pride over the

glossy commercial brand any day. a constantly inventing what we desire pride.

(with acknowledgements to adrienne rich whose words help close this piece)

open the brutal

open the brutal. your ghost in my machine.
my still eye in your hurricane. rupture
abundance. loosen the tyranny of the literal.
slippage is better than nothing, squirrel running
across the grass, a living question mark bouncing
black & feisty before my eyes. keep moving like
that squirrel, faster than the guard dog chasing it.
change the shape of the slot slide it somewhere
looser. your teeth a serif that hooks my ear.
loose hair flutters debris in the night. lyric is
not rule but desire. signpost the revolution.
your body's alphabet encrypts the message.
rising on the silent letter that changes the sound
around it. a woman's flesh with light blue roads
winding just below skin, how a small wrinkle holds
years in its fold, condenses time into her line of skin.
my line of vision.

storm

i don't follow & i don't lead. i was
never meant to dance in that strictly
defined way. body bobs upstarts its
own rhythms & upsets, small storms a
daily occurrence. yet somehow we
danced as though we could meet &
breathe the same air. your hand, my
back, like butter on bread, we were
morning familiar the moment we
met. click. in your presence i dance
on tabletops. click. can't follow you,
never could, you are like an
amputated arm, still feel your
presence long after your removal.
can't bandage this up. you instigate
the storms that move me along still.

take one

red bean black sesame paste baby comes
howling into this world learns to eat
every grain of rice her first english
word is no. NO. born with a serious
streak the width of an altar, she
watches soya beans squeezed in a rough
cotton bag, milk from her mother's
workworn hands. faith hides in little
pockets like the heart & the throat. the
leap of faith into english an ocean in
which many have drowned. her
internal life flourishes at the risk of the
external, always keep one eye to the
outer world, the way one fears and
respects a hungry tiger, the way dancer
& dance live in our rapidly thrilling
throats, filling each moment to the
fingertips.

chaos feary
(upon reading biopiracy by vandana shiva)

pyre in pirate bio in bile
mono in poly breeder in
womb pull of landrace allo
me poietic auto me diverse
trans over genic harassment
over seas genetic as pathetic
as engine of disease socio
me catastrophe political and
eugenic organ as an ism
general as the mono startle
of a soma ethic under
trodden patent as in lies
hubris as in corporate
culture as in american
military as a choking tentacle
as pollution erodes these lines
no sense in food or rhyme
resistant as in herbicide or
people lost and found field a
factory dinner a roulette
conquest as in seeds hands as in fist

ricochet

when the ship leaves the harbour, she hears the vomitting below.
circling the ship, huge lanterns hanging from choppers. the ocean is
angry. no, she is angry & blames the ocean. i can't bear the weight of
history & i can't not bear it. when her clothes are burned, the stench
sounds like canaries trapped in her throat. she knows she must make
home up, tallying words & numbers into skeletons off which to hang
her coat. the ship has left the harbour. it's not coming back. if i never
see another ship again, it'll be too soon. when she yawns, the canaries
flutter their smallest feathers. her breath smells of worms. until the
melancholy becomes cholera, i do not know the name of this language.
the shadow in the periphery would like to enter this room. why turn
away? she only wants to rub her face against your faithless arm.
tremble. ache. her name is slow. you have waited for her for a long
time. why don't you look at her face? her gentle grimace. an anchor
cold inside your belly. you don't know what she calls for because your
ears are plugged against uterine howls of pain. when the dried clams
became bloody soup, i smelled the harbour.

in for a penny, pound of flesh. crush the ginger. palm against the
knife. smash the root wide open. her nostrils accept ginger. the air is
in the kitchen. always carry a back up plan. garlic. flashlights. codes
in case the cops are invading your privacy. until the root was smashed,
i didn't know the sound of breakage. broken further than you knew
you could. then break it again. the language that turns your verbs
into nouns. messy accidents. argue incessantly if you have nothing
better to do. noise levels are rising. be still my scared heart.

when the door opened, it was round. a moon. a woman in a moon.
her gates wide open. just like that. the thresholds more vomitting the
smells she refuses to name as if forgetting were its own solution. not a
door today but a window. what are you saving the door for? don't
you know that intruders are welcome? until the handcuffs appeared,
she thought this place was benign if deluded. when the ship left the

harbour something inside broke. there is no fixing this. the oceans will swell with prayers, flotsam landing in places you'll never see. you have more trust than you know what to do with. blessings & curses are cousins. her palm wide open. knife reverberates, tremor of her adamant tendons. when she looked up, the canaries had fluttered off to other homes. she was still piling up words like they were cages she could turn into nests. couldn't she learn from the birds? fractured like your entry into the language. why don't you pull the weeds out of your garden for the slugs to feed on? why does your grandmother keep sticking her hands in the crumbling earth? wary of her bony frame. sometimes you have to be approximate before you go precise. all intentions are dangerous. you know yet you still proceed. sharp objects cause bleeding. until i ate the sharp object, i didn't know it would slice the inside like so many question marks. hooks into syntax force of abortion. mammoth prints in the crumbling earth.

damage

people walk around in various states of damage. damaged goods.
mismanaged funds. poverty rampage in corporate attire. let them eat
mutual funds. the rate of interest is ejaculatory. eleven dribbles into two.
murderous profit margins. mowing the law. moaning the lost. manning
the last financial post. when did i become a commodity? a calamity?
indemnity? the trend to credit facilitates fascism. ATM: automatically
tracks movement, a totalitarian market, antagonize the machine & see
what happens. waiting for goliath. the slingshot has become a
teddybear catapault. slapsuits on everything from burgers to cartoon
mice. the disney empire no laughing matter, laughing master. lasting
mistakes. would kafka wear nikes? hand-me-down reeboks? a
profound mistrust of fashion is healthy. your insecurities are showing.
disco famulan gives me a headache. on a coca cola campus, you learn
crud. pepsi pisses me off. hasn't all that sugar caused enough damage
already? walk around in sodapop stupor, coca cola carnage. a big burp
would be a start. chapters chatters a tale of diminishing returns,
nonchalant dirge for small presses. moaning the lost while the laughing
master snickers. where's my slingshot?

reverb

hyper-capitalism is not just annoying but deadly

some dreams are trances

the american trance

annoyance is a warning signal

corporations eat the poor and spit out their bones

nisgaa land

the amount of weaponry corresponds accordingly with the level of guilt

obscene wealth is not earned but stolen

i counted sweatshops in vancouver's eastside until i got dizzy and fainted

assume spiritual plenitude—can you?

she stumbled through the mall in a consumerist trance
until she decided to slice up her credit card in time to the muzak

lubicon land

irresponsible displacement of imperialist guilt causes massive deaths is
psychobabble for: learn to share

fiscal this and fiscal that

hand over fist

market forces

the captains of industry don't feel guilty about wealth because they share
the guilt

uranium nightmares, cobalt collusion

rearrange molecules through thought not genetic engineering

coast salish land

prisons R not us

the violent expulsion of (un)foreign bodies from this nation-state indicates
a guilty conscience

a desert waiting for your wisdom

think potlatch

broke un girl

spill a moonful

underground un done ground

riven

broke un rapport

girl friday gone sumday

myth is currency

eczema to skin as asphalt to soil, girls with city complexes shun masters

obsess gone to abcess

this stress has economic undercurrents

cashino markets eat soil gorge human toil

only broke unwords left

TO THE BIRDS

I shut my eyes and all the world drops dead;
I lift my lids and all is born again.
(I think I made you up inside my head.)

—*Sylvia Plath*, Mad Girl's Love Song

    I called Donimo and asked her to pick me up at the airport even
though we had already agreed that that was too much like girlfriends,
and we were just dating. She thought it would be OK given the
circumstances.

    When I arrived, she was waiting for me in army pants and
combat boots: fresh picked blueberries slowly bursting in one hand,
staining her fingers purple, a slender stem of cream green orchids in
the other. I didn't cry.

    Driving through thick fog to my apartment she said how unusual
it was for there to be fog in Vancouver and when there was fog it
didn't usually stay so long. If someone asked me whether or not fog
was unusual for Vancouver I would not know the answer. Things like
that slip through my brain unrecorded, leave no trace. I kept thinking,
I only ever knew one person in our family who died. My family
doesn't get sick. We don't go to the hospital.

    I put on my long black dress and we went out, came home and
fucked on the kitchen floor. I told her I loved her.

    "That's incredible," she said, and bit my neck. "Amazing." She
wrapped her arms around me thin but strong like rope, like she was
tying me to her. I waited for her to say it back. I pointed out how hard

it can be to make yourself vulnerable and a lot of people feel uncomfortable saying I love you.

"I'm not scared to say 'I love you.' I don't love you."

I stared at her. "Well I guess that's it then."

"Why?" she said. "Who knows what will happen? I don't say things unless I'm sure they're true. I like you very much." It was four in the morning. She went home.

*

When I was about seven, my mother went to the hospital for an operation. Dad took me and my younger sister Hannah to visit her. Grey tiled hospital corridors ending in shadows—a memory or something I made up later? I wasn't upset, even though she was gone for quite awhile, and no one told me what the operation was for.

When my mother came back from the hospital, I was just very matter of fact, and at the beginning of a lifetime of saying things I wasn't supposed to say without realizing what other people would feel or think because of it.

"Did you miss me while I was gone?"

I thought for a minute, then looked up at her.

"Well, to tell the truth, Mommy," I answered, "I'd sort of forgotten about you."

She remembers that story even now, and still tells it, even though she really can only start the first sentence. Then someone else picks up where she left off, and she laughs when they get to the punch line. That bratty daughter of hers with the bookish vocabulary. She laughs, and then shakes her head and frowns, maybe remembering how it felt to be forgotten.

When I was a teenager she was in the hospital again, for surgery on a hernia. She told me and my sister how the doctors had found her mother's cancer during a hernia operation. Dad took us to visit her and I got so panicked at the sight of her in the bed and the smell of the hospital that I had to wait for my dad and Hannah outside in the parking lot. That was a few months after quitting candy striping because of the smell of the hospital cafeteria and my friend Jacky making me laugh when this guy in a wheelchair leaked piss all over the white tiled floor. I had to stop feeding him and go in the other room.

*

My first Vancouver basement suite had a carpeted kitchen. Dried bits of food nestled in the carpet, which had faded to a non-colour between grey and beige. In the bathroom, orange mushrooms grew on the shower ceiling, appearing suddenly from out of nowhere.

My round-faced boyfriend and I moved to Vancouver because we couldn't find jobs in Montreal and Vancouver seemed like a good place to try next. We didn't think about what it would be like to live there forever, across the world from our families in Fredericton, New Brunswick. Craig got a job in a bank soon after we arrived; every morning I would lie in bed and listen to the sounds of the coffee grinder and the electric razor. I felt like I was floating through time. No one was expecting me anywhere. It seemed like I could disappear without a trace.

That's when I had the dream—woke up and it was sticking to my face like spider threads:

My mother lost, wandering from room to room.

Wearing a flowered flannel nightgown, she floated away from me in a cloud of blue.

I still have the picture I drew the next morning. Chalk pastels. Blurred.

It never occurred to me to go back home because I hated the city where my parents had ended up. I couldn't breathe there. Their ending up in Fredericton was as arbitrary as me ending up in Vancouver but I kept thinking they could have made a better choice. They could have chosen a place with people like us: dark, Jewish, politically left-wing, outsiders. Instead they chose a bleached white province on the east coast of Canada, filled with pale people like my boyfriend's family, who had lived there for generations and generations.

Not long after I moved to Vancouver, I told my mother about my new friends. They were all feminists, and almost all lesbians, working in the movement to end violence against women. I told my mother how much I liked these women, how I even wished I could be one of them, except for the fact that I had a boyfriend.

"I can imagine that it would be great to hang around with people who had gone through the process of . . ." She paused.

"Coming out?"

"Yes. You'd have to think about your life in a way that most of us don't ever have to."

Not long after, I called to tell them that I was a lesbian. I had hoped it would be more dramatic, but it felt like a small happening, a natural result of my boyfriend moving out and all my friends being lesbians. "We thought you already told us this," said my parents.

Six years after the chalk pastel dream, in the taxi on the way to the airport, I watched the city go by; Vancouver had started to feel like home. I had moved out of my last basement suite, gotten a job that kept me rooted in time and space, kept me from floating.

That was the summer that my mother began to disappear.

My friend Adriane says that I first started noticing things a year earlier when they visited me on the way home from Alaska. Adriane and I drove down to Seattle to pick them up at SeaTac, found my mom by the baggage carousel. And now I seem to remember that she looked lost, that when I asked where my father was she wasn't sure. But is that just me adding things back in to a memory full of holes?

And is this something else I made up: some time after that visit a midnight call home in the middle of a nasty breakup, strung out from not eating or sleeping. In my late twenties, I still called them in the middle of the night to cry and hear them murmur sleepy comfort. They always picked up the phone. But that time there was something different. Like Mom wasn't sure what was wrong when I called. Maybe she was just tired of listening to me. Something did happen to me after that though, maybe a preparation for what was to come. In the middle of freaking out about the dramatic end of another unlikely relationship, a suspicion that I needed to grow up and get on with things. A realization that all my losses so far had been relatively minor.

*

The first time I saw Donimo was at a women-only strip show in a sleazy downtown bar. An empty, waiting space surrounded her, separated her from the other women there. She chooses and wears her clothes deliberately; that night it was a narrow black suit: pants low on her hipbones, tight down to steel toed boots. The cuffs of her shirt covered her hands in a dandyish way, grazing her precise artists' fingers and her dime store ring. Bad, said the one she was wearing. Her other one says Sick. Her gaze is not easily distracted once she has been interested.

We knew enough people in common for me to invite her to my birthday party, the fifth Gemini party that I had co-hosted; my friend's house near Trout Lake was crowded with drunk people. When I was hiding in the bathroom to escape all the people, trying to re-apply my lipstick, I heard her voice. I opened the door and saw her approaching, then shut it again and tried to feel a little less drunk. When I opened the door again, she was talking to people in the hall; she looked up at me. In one hand she held a plate of fruit cut in thin slices and arranged in concentric circles, a small dish of something creamy in the middle. In her other hand she carried a box wrapped in copper coloured paper.

"Where should I put these?"

She was all angles and boots and heavy rings again but because we weren't in the bar I noticed how blue her eyes were; her blue eyes and blonde hair and slightly pink cheeks seemed at odds with the edges of the rest of her, though her hair was spiked and her eyes travelled slowly over my small dress.

It's hard to keep your composure when you are drunk and also very attracted to someone. I took the plate of fruit over to the food table full of chips and salsa, hummus and pita. I was learning that she is in some ways more of a gay man than a lesbian, a faithful consumer of Gourmet magazine, who keeps her boots polished and places great stock in manners. When she wasn't looking I put my finger into the cream in the small dish, tasted honey.

When I came back to her she asked, "And this?" holding up the gift.

I took it from her.

"Thanks. You didn't have to get me anything."

As I turned to take the gift into the bedroom, "It's customary," she said, "to open the gift in front of the gift-giver."

Hannah called me the next day.

"Something's wrong with Mom. Ever since she lost her job she's been acting really weird." I said that of course Mom was acting weird. After working for the provincial government for years, developing kindergarten curriculum, integrating children with disabilities into the mainstream schools, she'd been cut along with half of her department.

"It might be good to get back to teaching kindergarten," she had said at the time. "That's what I really love." But even though she worked hours and hours of overtime, she had trouble making lesson plans, keeping the classroom organized, controlling the wilder kids. Partway through the year, under pressure from parents, she resigned.

"She's really depressed," insisted Hannah. And she won't talk to anyone. She thinks she might be starting menopause but she won't go to the doctor."

I called home, talked to my mother about doctors, about finding a woman doctor her age, since she thought her young male doctor was a twit. "I could help you when I get back." "OK," she said.

On our first date, Donimo's white shirt fell open at the neck, revealing the sharpness of her collarbone and the shadows that curved in the hollow of her throat. I took her out to dinner and I was surprised to find us talking. We talked about our childhoods, coming out, art, music.

"I brought dessert," she said, "But it must be eaten somewhere scenic."

We drove to Sunset Beach and sat on a bench looking out over the ocean, and she took a small box of handmade chocolates from the inside breast pocket of her suit and gave me a bite of one for every secret I told her.

"But I want to know secrets about you too."

"You don't have anything to bargain with," she said. That's how I got to kiss her for the first time.

In Fredericton a few weeks later I tried to talk to Mom about the doctor but she got impatient and said she didn't need to see any doctor. I started to cry and her reaction was something I never would have anticipated. Instead of reassuring me, she looked at Dad in confusion.

"Rob, Sarah's crying because I won't go to the doctor."

It started like that. Small things.

She would forget to close the car door after she got out. Vibrate like a trapped moth behind the screen door in the kitchen instead of following the rest of us outside. Dad or I cooked supper while she opened drawers, got out spoons and knives, looked at them and put them back.

I still have a photograph on my desk from that first summer, to remind me of the beginning: a photograph of her with her worm composter taken for my collection: Mom kissing the cat, Mom crunching into the season's first apple, Mom leaning back in her favourite chair, laughing. Dad in the sweater he'd knitted. Both of them working in the garden. I always kept every picture I took of my parents, maybe in an attempt to erase the geographical distance between us.

Mom squatted down beside the container of red wrigglers for the photo, smiling softly, loving her worms just for eating kitchen scraps. When I visit her now, that seems to be the core of her, as the rest is stripped away: a strangely simple and old-fashioned love for animals, plants, children, anything small. When the photograph was developed, I was surprised at how strained her smile was, how her eyebrows were raised as if to ask a stranger, *What are you doing? What do you want?*

Dad's family was visiting that summer and Mom wouldn't tell anyone what was wrong, kept saying she was OK, got confused or angry if we kept asking. She knew everyone was talking about her behind her back; cousins and aunts pushed into my room to ask what was wrong with Mom, until they'd used up all the oxygen. I held my breath and waited for them to leave. I didn't know anything more than they did.

The iron plugged in, scorching the air; wrinkled clothes piled beside it. Mom standing in the garden, a handful of weeds crushed in her hand.

"The iron was on? Oh dear…" She looked around at the flowers and vegetables. Breathing in the smell of tomatoes in August sun, I waited for her to tell me why she had forgotten the iron. Waited for her to get angry. Finally she glanced up at me. "Look at these roses; isn't that just the perfect red?"

In the guest room that used to be my room I sat on the bed and wondered what to do. Childhood pictures surrounded me: my sister and me at the edge of a field in clothes Mom had made us, dresses just like Laura's and Mary's from *Little House on the Prairie*. A black and white close-up of my mother holding me, her gaze intent and focused on my newborn face. The photograph was not so much a picture of me or of her as it was a record of her connection to me, the force of her presence in my world. As I stared at the picture I felt her arms release me, her eyes lose their focus; felt her turning away.

*

In the mid-sixties, my city-born parents lived on an island off the coast of Maine; my father taught five children in the one room school. After I was born, we moved to Boston, and two years later when my sister was an infant, we arrived in a small town in eastern Maine, a sparse collection of houses scattered along a dirt road. My parents rented a century-old farmhouse with peeling yellow paint and unfinished floors.

Our cat got used to her new home right away, presenting us with small warm mouse bodies, dead or half dead, waiting until we praised her to begin eating. She left only the entrails, gleaming like small jewels. The landlady owned most of the town. She only rented the house to us, not the land—orchards of twisted apple trees, sweet fields of long grass we tunnelled in until the end of the summer, when her drunk boyfriend came to cut the hay. The barn was slowly collapsing. Clinging tight to the rope swing, Hannah and I learned to jump from the highest loft, up into the dusty dark and then down, the abrupt landing in itchy hay. We ran and climbed trees and turned over rocks to find bugs, slid our fingers into the silky mud that forms when puddles on a dirt road dry out in mid-summer.

Mom showed me the best way to kill slugs.

You go into the garden with your scissors and go clip clip clip.

My mother has always had a deep reverence for living creatures.

But slugs are an exception.

Slugs are cruel, she insists, the way they eat tender green shoots in spring, or chew through sunflowers in August, sunflowers that have spent months growing tall and strong.

Mom gritted her teeth as we hunted through the rows of vegetables, bending down and turning over leaves.

"But don't cut the baby ones, OK, Mommy? Or they'll cry."

"Oh dear, I suppose it's not a very nice thing to do, is it?"

She didn't take me with her after that.

As I grew older, the age and history of our house overwhelmed me, the traces of the family who built it, relatives of the landlady. What would it be like to live forever in the same place you'd been born, the same place your parents and grandparents and generations before that had been born and lived and died? The man who had built the house stared at me and my sister from a sepia-tinted photo, his eyes following us no matter where we went. Old furniture and odds and ends were piled high in one room, antiques mixed with yellowed comic books. Hannah and I hid in there, and once, knowing that no adult would ever come into the corner where I played, I peed on the floor, watching the yellow puddle spread and then stay still, its edges drying in the close hot air. The next day the puddle had disappeared, no trace of me left.

My parents have a photograph of me taken when I was newly six, headed to school for my first day. In the picture I am smiling wide, gripping my lunchbox, standing straight and tall as possible. I wear the polyester suit my mother bought me for school, red and green plaid, brass buttons. I had worn that suit all summer, climbing the knotty apple trees and crawling through the tunnels we made under the raspberry bushes. I was in love with that suit and what it promised.

My father took the photograph. Then my mother drove me, in our blue VW bug, down the dirt road to Clark Avenue Elementary, where one hundred students, grades one through eight, awaited me. All strangers. The fresh eagerness of the girl in the photo must have drained out through my toes, spilled out of the hole in the floor of our car onto the dusty road as we drove.

By the time we got to the square white school I was sobbing, clinging to the handle of the car door, my stomach lurching as I was faced with the reality, the inevitability, of my mother's parting. I filled up the air in the little round car with my crying. I cried all the way into the school, my mother beside me holding my hand. There was no way to stave off the mornings that lined up ahead of me, the days and days of my mother leaving.

In my bedroom at the end of the upstairs hall the fat white flowers on the wallpaper gleamed in the night, changed shape. The sheets on my heavy-footed bed were always cold, too cold for me to extend my legs all the way, and besides there were unknown crawling things down at the bottom. Inside the walls the squirrels ran and ran. And there were always mice, in spite of our hunter.

I woke up screaming a lot. Nightmares.

My mother like Miss Clavel: her nightgown streaming behind, running fast, and faster.

I'd wake up just before I began screaming.

That moment when the dream still lingered at the edge of my bed. Knowing she would come.

She'd run down the hall. I pretended to be screaming in my sleep, so she'd wake me up. Stroke my hair.

Every house we lived in, she ran to me.

*

"Dad, we have to talk to Mom." The day after I found the iron he and I were finally alone together, getting groceries at the new Superstore. Mom tried to walk here a few days ago, but got lost somewhere in the five blocks between the house and the store, came home empty-handed and quiet.

"What do you want to talk to her about?" He put a bag of granny smiths in the cart. "These are Mom's favourites." I watched him scan the rest of the fruit aisle, my throat tightening as I saw how grey he'd gotten, his face more lined than I remembered. He wasn't asking for an answer, only keeping up his side of the conversation. It made him seem absent-minded, but I suspected some part of him was knowingly evading me.

"Dad—"

"What sweetie?"

"Something's wrong with Mom." He sighed, pushed the grocery cart down the aisle a few feet. I waited. Finally his answer, delivered in pieces, as if it was too exhausting to say all at once.

"Well. She's had a hard year. Losing her job last winter. Maybe—maybe she's a little depressed. Should we get peaches or nectarines?"

My answer came fast, indignant. "She forgets things. She left the iron on. It's dangerous."

"Oy, honey, when you get to be our age, you forget things."

"But Mom's always had a good memory. And you guys are only 53."

"Oy."

Now he tells me that Oy has become his refrain; he feels like he is always sighing. I persisted, not used to his tiredness yet, fighting against what seemed like faint-hearted avoidance. "And she does weird things. Sometimes it's like she can't figure out how to open the door, or answer the phone."

"Yeah. I know. God, the price on this blue cheese."

"You know?"

"Yes, I know." He looked at me for the first time since I started this discussion. "Things have been happening since the spring. It's not like I haven't noticed."

We looked at each other, another beginning: a connection between us that does not include her; something that, in her bitter moments, she sees as conspiracy, and that reminds her of the times when my sister and I were children that she would accuse us of loving Dad more than we loved her. It was because we were girls she said; boys favour their mothers.

"Did you ever ask her what's wrong?"

He looked away again and steered the cart towards the checkout counter. "I tried. She just gets so angry. It's embarrassing for her."

"Maybe we could try to talk to her together."

"She really hates the idea that people are talking about her."

"Come on Dad, we can just tell her we're worried about her."

"We could try. Look at these avocados. They're rock hard. You must get good avocados in Vancouver."

The whole time I was at my parents' house I was distracted by the heat between me and Donimo, the emails, the phone calls in the middle of the night, the things she had given me to remind me of her while we were apart. She is a careful and formal person. I had never slept in her bed; would leave her apartment wild-eyed at four in the morning rather than fall into the intimacy of shared sleep. I called her that night. She told me then about her mother and the months she'd spent visiting her at Riverview Psychiatric Hospital. The long drives there and back, the music she blasted to keep herself on the road. When I said I thought there was something wrong with my mother's brain she made no move to contradict me or reassure me that nothing was wrong.

Hannah had just moved out of my parents' house and was angry at Mom for acting strange, had few feelings of sympathy. She told me how Mom had stormed up the stairs one Saturday afternoon before Hannah moved out. "One pair of footwear only in the front hall!" She came into Hannah's room and threw the offending extra shoes on the floor.

"What?" said Hannah.

"It's the rule! One pair of shoes per person can be left downstairs! The rest of your shoes get put away in your room!" Mom clomped back down the stairs. Hannah came down a while later.

"Hello, sweetie," said Mom. "Having a relaxing afternoon?"

Dad and I waited until Hannah had left for the summer before we talked to Mom. We weren't angry like she was: Dad was just impatient. I wasn't angry at all then.

She came with us into the living room, but she wouldn't sit down, just shifted from one foot to the other. A thick tree swaying, the wind tearing away leaves. My plane was leaving that night; Vancouver was waiting for me: my tiny attic apartment, blue mountains resting just outside my window. The first time I'd been able to picture it since I'd been here.

My mother, no longer the mild lover of animals, glared at my father. "You're getting to be just like your sisters, Rob. You can't let people be."

He adjusted the blinds hanging crooked in the window. Rice paper blinds with long tangled cords; I could never get them to roll up straight.

"Midge, we just want to help."

"Everybody talking about what's wrong with me. I hate it." She rubbed her hands together, shivered. "It's so cold in here."

"We just want to help." Dad sat down, looked at his hands. Only half of him in the room, the rest somewhere else. Where this was not happening. As he faded, I felt myself becoming heavier, sinking into my family for the first time in years.

"Mom, please don't be mad." I moved towards her. "Maybe we could just talk a little."

She was still shivering in the July heat and I went to close the door to the garden.

Behind me, a choking noise, then, "Can you get me some toilet paper?"

Turning around I saw her lip was trembling and a clear drop hung from her nose. She used to embarrass us so much when we were kids; her nose dripped in the cold, and she'd curl her tongue right up to catch the snot. "I'm just lucky to have such a long tongue," she'd say.

The thin white paper crumpled in her hands. Her hands with their heavy blue veins; the jade wedding ring. "My first wedding ring turned my finger green," she told us. "Dad made it for me in his art class, some kind of wire."

She wiped her eyes and blew her nose. Slowly lowered herself onto the couch, at the opposite end from where Dad hunched. He reached out and touched her arm, then pulled himself back in. I sat down across from them.

My mother rolled the damp toilet paper into a ball, looked out the window at the roses, then back down at the carpet.

"I have Alzheimers."

This was not a prophecy, though she knew something was wrong. It was an incantation, an invocation: naming the evil to prevent it from coming. A traditional practice in our family.

Dad rubbed his head, sighed. Looked up at her. "You do not have Alzheimers." His need for rest, for quiet, for the wind to die down.

I knew he was using the wrong strategy. *Shhh, quiet. Don't interrupt her prayer. It won't work if you contradict it, recklessly assume the best.*

My mother spoke again. "I forget things all the time. And it takes so long to finish anything." Then she turned to me. "My mother died so young. Her life's work, her writing. Unfinished."

The blue mountains rose again in my mind; with effort I turned back towards the east. *Try to calm her without breaking the spell.* "Mom. You don't know. Please. You don't know. It's been a hard year."

They were both looking at me, listening. I took a deep breath, spoke slowly. "Talk to a counsellor, Mom. Have some tests. We'll find out what's wrong."

My mother took my hand and stroked it. My father moved closer to her on the couch.

My mother looked out the window towards the garden. "The roses this year. I've never seen them so brilliant."

Dad stood up. "We better eat dinner if you want to catch your plane."

*

Dear Mom,

I am so glad we talked. I love you. You will be fine.

*

Nouns fall out of sentences.

Cupboard doors hang open.

Children's paintings pile high on teacher's empty desk, slide down, drift to the floor.

*

The psychologist showed my mother tiny drawings of families in houses, in parks, at the beach, then hid the pictures and asked her questions about them. Recorded her responses on his clipboard.

"Why does he need to ask so many questions? Who cares about his stupid little forms?"

The naturopath said many things could be cured with herbs; she gave my mother St John's wort for depression and gingko for memory.

"Now that is a lovely young woman."

Mom spent hours taking all the clothes out of her dresser, folding and unfolding them, putting them in her suitcase, taking them out, putting them in again. Dad ended up packing both suitcases himself. Then they went to Mexico for the year. It was Dad's sabbatical.

The roles of parent and child had always been clear in my family. It felt strange to worry about them. I called them more than I expected.

"How are you Mom?"

"Well, I've made a chart of all my pills and when I'm supposed to take them. I think that's helping."

For some reason I never got charged for any of the calls I made to Mexico. They just didn't appear on my phone bills.

At winter solstice Donimo and I spent the weekend together. As I was lying with my head on her chest, her ribs hard against my cheek, she said my name. I didn't answer because I always like to hear her say my name. Her thin fingers curled in my hair, she said my name again. And then she told me she loved me.

My brain which usually spins and spins slowly quieted and I felt the sheets and her body warm around me, felt all of the places where our bodies touched, even the curls of my hair wound tight in her hand.

HASTINGS PARK

origin is unoriginal
not a beginning
                simply a point
on a line
                with stories behind and stories ahead

Prologue

In the poempark   the seasons spill
as one.
Each line: a tree planted,
grows roots; the roots tunnel beneath the page.
Limbs stem.

Occasionally, a small shudder
is a thought misremembered.

*

The poempark is domestic.
Words carefully placed and arranged assemble.
A wilderness.

At night, the howl of beasts   (imagined)

keeps us awake.
*

The poempark has no river running through it
for at times the poempark is itself
a river.

*

The poetarchitect considers the poempark. In their mind's eye
this lasts seconds   or a century.
Then, in a sudden furious burst   (always unexpected)
the poetarchitect draws the poem. Into a park.
Writes the park. Into a poem.

A void bordered.

*

Some days, visitors
flood the gates in hoards.   Enticed.

Then for months   the park, exposed to the elements, waits.
                                                                Neglected.
A barely tangible breeze stirs the grass,
reminds the park   that it is indeed.

from Origins or The Book of Questions

Is risking an act of

morning, the sunrise between sleep
a lily
        breaking?

The book is thick.
If filled with words
will it be thicker?

If a questionmark didn't

the possibility of a question
its existence
its wolfishness

In this book there are no keys.

In one beginning (1889)   if dates are needed
the park has a vision.

The park shall be   a park.

Major Oppenheimer   *a constant resort for all lovers*
                    of romantic woodland scenery and lovely groves.

If dates need twenty years
the vision dulls
                    sharp knife carves
a pleasure garden
                    now blunt instrument
blade-rust in the open grave of the park.

Cataract of buildings, stadiums,
parking lots, livestock, fairs,
busy men and women scrambling
(so much to do and see), success
and industry.

The park becomes a beggar   roots-rusted   anxious
assuring passer-byes that once
it was   a park.

*

In the building of a book
there are techniques
one must learn
to keep wolves out.
Early morning   have the blinds drawn in the east
                     and open in the west.

Afternoon reverses.

Though the windows stay shut
all day long.

*

A slaughterhouse built in haste.   A new city demands meat.
                                     A city will have its meat.

A slaughterhouse built
because it can't be helped.

1869   Land Auction, New Westminster
Lot #26   purchased
George Black   buyer
The Slaughterhouse   a shack

boarded with rough lumber, hand-split cedar roof

He casts his lot
twenty five down, twenty five later
not exactly game
but a land of hemlock
and swamp, cedar and scrub.

                        1863

The land, lacking
pioneers, has to be   divided
                         and numbered.

A piece of forest
with a small stream   lot number 26.

A meaningless equation
perfectly understood
in pioneer language.

This is not a riddle.
A place you go to find laughter. Thick,
abundant. Laughter you can hold
in your hands. Laughter   you can laugh at.

This, a slaughterhouse
built over a stream.
The stream blushing into Burrard Inlet.

*

Is the slaughterhouse a confession?
The fire pit out back a mouth left open?
The pulley and hook the ghost of a word? The word of a ghost.

*

A word can travel back in time, invent its origin, its muse.

Hastings Mills, Hastings Street, Hastings Park, Hastings
Hotel, Hastings Townsite, Rear Admiral George Fowler
Hastings, Khanamoot.

*

Here Vancouver began. All was forest towering to the skies. British Royal
Engineers surveyed it into lots and everything began . . .
　　　　　　　　　　(from a commemorative plaque located at New Brighton)

Clam beach, cedar forest peopled,
bear-ridden. Musqueam feet used.
The knotted, dewy ground gave
them a trail. A mark.

And a name appeared, Khanamoot.
This verb borne more than itself.
The act. The name brought
familiarity, use, ties, a home.

Soon a new trail followed the original.
A game of cat and mouse. A game?
Sturdy planks of wood covered
the footpath. Long enough to fit

the largest carriages trailing
to Khanamoot, now New Brighton,
the most fashionable watering place
in BC. (For months you could still see

footprints between the cracks.)
Along the planks a long list
of firsts settled (though awkwardly
fitted): the first post office, customs,

bridge, the first hotel, stable, telegraph,
the first dock, ferry, playing field,
CPR Office, the first museum.
You see, the century had turned

and firsts became important, you
might even say, an obsession.

George Black, a worldly man, doesn't begin
with cattle and meat
but with a seaside resort.   1865

                                    Down the stream,
                                    (later the red stream, later pushed
underground to make way
for horse racing and roller-coasters)   ocean-side,
                                    Brighton Hotel is built.

A hotel and a slaughterhouse. And a stream in between.
Black new to this wilderness. This coast. And him not looking back.

Of course, as usual in these sort of circumstances,
the smell is a problem.
Also the cattle skulls, the bones.

*

inwards stories are foreign
render the skin puckered
pulley and hook
                    a park with no history
cattle hung by my open mouth
& blood is draining   a little to fast

When he dies
Black relinquishes a few heirlooms: a plank road
                                        a burned hotel
                                        & a widow.

The widow has nightmares.
At night
she strolls the Scottish countryside,
mouth filled
with sweet scent of broom.
But when she wakes
                                Oh sorrow!
                                This cursed coast!
Nothing   but moss,
                    young mountains
                    and eight months of rain.

Water   diligent
works on the soil   loosens
                                and the soil drains.

Surely this is an ever encroaching ocean
tide always coming
never going
                            Where is that spit of sand
                            she swears she saw
                            ten years back.
                            And the forest,
                            once looming,
                            now dead logs hug the shore.

The widow panics.
She digs out old storybooks,
reads instructions about the Arc
and sells the five acre lot

to the BC Gas and Electrical Company
for one hundred and fifty thousand dollars.
The same day, she books a train to Halifax
and a cabin on the first ship
back to paradise.

    *

How to invent this man?   The slaughterhouse fire pit,
What shudders at the root of a story? now merely an idea.
What shudders at the root of him?   Long filled in, closed up, built over
Need? Before language.   a child's ferris wheel,
                             an army barrack,
a red, red barn.

In the red barn, the cement floor gives way in places
                    to uneven lumps,
                    floor slightly raised.

Beneath—a resting place for cattle bones, stories petrified.

This is George Black's legacy.

Each year the bones work themselves
closer to the surface, threaten
                to break through.

The caretaker (mute by childhood) signs to park officials.
Something must be done.

    *

Childhood has gypsy fairs
not recollected in tranquillity
but hardly recollected.

to try dizzying   I have been almost as closed
                                         and final as a book.

Childhood is gypsy fairs
squatting on barren land   trampled

swings twirling like the gypsy women's skirts
multicoloured balls, whistles, string,
red and green popcorn, and pink cotton candy,
fake pipes, plastic bracelets, rings
and dark faces   so many dark faces

childhood is fairs
gypsying

grandmother crossing the canal
hating gypsies
                          crossing the canal
to buy a bunch of cherries, stems tied
with string.

(Come in under the shadow of this red rock)
and . . . I will show you fear in a handful of dust.
I will show you longing in a blade of grass
longing which, with a steady rake, the caretaker
gathers each fall and spring.

*

"Never   spirit of the west,   brook no obstacle
              the Hastings Park   carven
        heart of   forest wilderness,   critical
citizen and visitor is   exhibition and playground,   nature
eminent fitted   the most   kind   west . . .

          a short while ago   nothing   densest   woods defy   the
hand of man   change   the primeval   now   manufacturers
        east   west,   north   south   display   their wares
     commodious   livestock   all   on exhibition   crowds of
throbbing humanity pour   along the 'skid road', the future,
                     removed from the first condition of things."

*

(from Vancouver *Daily News – Advertiser*, Aug. 16, 1910)

The caretaker, a man who shuffles
and talks to birds with his hands, is ageless.
When a child. Lost his age and voice,
let them go, paper boats released in the flow of a stream.

He, a window, mirror, tunnel.
He, where the story begins
for this is a story of heartbreak and he is heartbreak.

The caretaker. A man. Who shuffles
and talks to birds. With his hands is ageless.
When a child lost his age and voice.
Let them go. Paper boats released in the flow. Of a stream.

The caretaker doesn't measure time.
Hours, useless. At the bottom of the pond
he can see the building that once stood there.

Now the stream has been surfaced.
He follows the water to its origin.
Begins his descent.

There are walls. They surround him.
Honks, buzz and tire screech, an errant gunshot
and horses' hooves in the gravel, laughter and whirr
of machines, water frolicking in a concrete fountain.

feria   rips   open
    lies exposed
              the park's red heart
   beating on the muddy earth

       Through this door, ladies and gents,
       the petrified woman awaits.
       Are you a doctor sir? A scientist perhaps?
       Step this way and see the wonders of the universe.

feria   loses itself in crowds
   pleads with strangers
   Explain me

       Come one, come all, and marvel
       at Independence, our educated horse.
       That's right, a human brain! She will amuse you,
       amaze you. Just drop your nickel in the box.

feria   isn't light
            as fairies

pale, fair, nor impartial

this word won't talk to birds

       They'll whirl and sway, give you a wink
       or two. Our Orientals and Salome Dancers, Spanish Carmens
       & genuine Dutch comedians. Leave your kids
       at the merry-go-rounds. Come to the Great Burlesque!

meaning fair-game
             vulnerable
feria

bursts with secrets

Straight from the ancient land of spices
and dark beauties, from the river Ganges
to the New World, the Sacred Crocodile sacrificed
200 years ago, now on display for your viewing pleasure.

feria   lonesome
  needs spectators
  storms inhabit this word
*
A woman approaches with a speech
of disused tongues. What sort of speech shall she fashion?

She divides the park
into four languages.

One for a whole season of doubts.
Doubt in a pencil's broken end. Doubt in the grass-growing
cracks of the tennis court, the half-torn fence.
Doubt in the red barn empty with picnic tables stacked roof-high,
the terrible stalls (echo of horses with no horses).

A second as a season of oracles.
In a dormitory a woman inconsolably wailing.
A straw bouquet.
On the rocky beach a sign
stumbled up to years later. (The paper mill.)
A second sign contradicting the first.
In a dormitory a woman. Inconsolably wailing.

Finally, a game.

The third for a day.
The one day in a year when she discloses his hand.
The remaining three hundred and sixty four days slowly forget
all answers tempered in his palm.

And the last. A carnival.

interest in fine arts, horticulture, women's
work,   cattle, sheep and swine   cage birds,
    ,   ,   , minerals, school
            Exhibition.   depart
the greater   number   exhibits come   citizen   is
hobbies,   interests,   business.
the other fellow   anxious   where he
stands,   held   separate
     so   shown

                 held.

         industrial exhibitor   can be summed up in a
few words   space

               space

            space
       space every year   from the very first,
we think we say all that is necessary."

(excerpts from the Vancouver Exhibition Association, 1925)

Vancouver, a hollowed history.
City on the edge of a continent. All margins. All geography.

A park on the edge of the city, geography stripped
bare, becomes. Or a story minus the beginning.

The park invents.
A pulley & hook for a muse.

13 RESOLUTE ROAD

Sister Beatrice taught third grade.
I was in second grade.
But next year,
she would be my teacher.

Chain link stretched high,
over my head.

Fenced the playground like a cage.

Sister Beatrice stood guard at the gate, back up against the fence, arms folded across her chest. She never moved, never smiled, never took her eyes off kids, during recess.

No one passed through the gate without her permission.
She only let kids out to go to the bathroom.

Kids lined up at the front door,
down the steps of the little school.

A line for the boys.
A line for the girls.

Sister Leah stood by in the hall watching who went in and who came out of the bathrooms. Every once in a while she poked her head in the door. When someone took too long. Checked they did not run the faucet, waste water, play with pink powder soap, wet paper towels.

Sister Leah sent them back outside to play.

There were rules.

Do not take one step off the blacktop onto the grass.
"Grass muddies shoes. Grass stains uniforms."

Do not climb or hang on the fence.
"We don't want people driving by in cars to think our school is a zoo."

No fighting.
"We should ALL get along as good Christians."

Girls are not allowed to hang upside down on the monkey bars.
"Unless shorts or tights are worn to cover undergarments."

Boys are not allowed to peek under a girl's uniform skirt.
"Boys might be tempted to sin."

Boys are not allowed to chase after girls.
"Boys might be tempted to sin."

It happened the last week of second grade. In the middle of afternoon. Right before recess. The whole class was reading. Sister Ima stepped out of the room, closing the door behind. She left us alone. She was gone a long time.

Jennifer Loftus tossed a beanbag across the desk row.

A yellow frog beanbag.

She kept it hidden in a dark corner of her desk.

Green polka dots.
Black button eyes.
Red felt tongue.

William Netson caught it, tossed it back.
"Give it here."
"No, give it here."
Open hands reached out for it, up and down the desk rows.

William Netson was going to throw it to Jackie Enwright drooling and waving his arms at the back of the class, but he faked it and tossed the yellow frog beanbag across the room.

"Give it back!" Jennifer Loftus swung around in her seat.

Bobby Columble, the shortest boy, laughed and petted the back of the yellow frog. Held it up to his lips. Gave it a kiss. Made a sick face, slumping over in his seat like he was dying. The whole class laughed and he sat up and tossed the yellow frog high in the air.

The yellow frog beanbag as high as the ceiling.

Legs dangling.

William Netson caught it as Sister Ima stepped through the door. The whole class grabbed up their books. I tried to find the place where I left off.

Sister Ima. She puffed up like a pufferbelly fish, barged down the desk row, snatched up the yellow frog beanbag away from William Netson.

He jumped up out of his seat, pointing a finger at Jennifer Loftus. "It's her beanbag. She threw it first!"
"Sit!"
"Down!"

Sister Ima yelled.

William Netson shrank back into his seat. Sat down. He glared across the desk row at Jennifer Loftus, sitting quiet, with her head down reading her book, as if she had nothing to do with what was going on.

Sister Ima, filling up the space between them, held the yellow frog beanbag out in front of Jennifer Loftus.

"This is yours?" she asked.

William Netson hung on the back of his chair, wearing a smirk on his face; pleased someone besides him was getting in trouble. And Jennifer Loftus stared at the yellow frog beanbag in the palm of Sister Ima's hand. She didn't look at Sister Ima, didn't say anything. Just looked sad at the yellow frog beanbag. Sister Ima knew it was hers. Sister Ima made and sold the beanbags at the spring bazaar to raise money for the school. Jennifer Loftus bought it with her allowance. I was there. I was there with her when she bought the yellow frog beanbag.

Jennifer Loftus nodded.

The yellow frog beanbag plopped on the desk.

"It's not fair!" William Netson shouted. "It's not fair!"

But Sister Ima didn't care, didn't listen.

"Put it away." She said to Jennifer Loftus. "At the end of the day, take it home with you. Don't ever let me see it again."

"It's not fair! You're not supposed to play favorites!"

William Netson stood up to her back.

Sister Ima straightened.

"Young Man." She said turning, towering over him, "You are missing recess." Her finger wagged in his face. "Even if she threw the beanbag *you* should have the maturity not to be distracted, *nor* to distract the rest of your classmates. You could have chosen to ignore the first toss. Now, I've had enough outbursts. Sit down!"

Sister Ima waited for his next move, but William Netson stood there in a daze repeating the words over in his head. His lips were moving, but no sound was coming out. Then he stopped, all of a sudden slamming his fist down on top of his desk and landing in his seat so hard I could feel the wall next to my desk shake.

Sister Ima lifted her gaze, to look around the room at the rest of the class.

Heads shot down.

Sunshine.

Blue sky.

Jennifer Loftus didn't have to stay inside at all. Even if it was her beanbag. Even if she started the beanbag toss.

I felt sorry for William Netson. He was always getting in trouble. Couldn't remember to raise his hand before asking a question. Just stood up in his chair and blurted out whatever he had to say. Had to be reminded ALL the time—chairs were for sitting, not for standing.

Halfway through recess he came through the gate.

Sister Ima must have let him out.

Jackie Enwright, Bobby Columble saw him. They called him over. But William Netson didn't even turn his head. It was like he didn't see or hear them.

William Netson walked into the middle of the playground, walked right past everyone playing around him. His eyes glued on the other side of the playground. I watched him coming towards me, arm hanging, fingers curling. I watched him walk straight past me. Then I knew. I wasn't very far away. He walked right up to Jennifer Loftus, stood inches from her face.

You bitch.

I heard him.
I heard him say those words.
Those were his exact words.
William Netson said those exact words.

Jennifer Loftus.
Her open mouth, white blonde braids, hanging down past her shoulders.

I wasn't standing far away.

Sister Beatrice. Her black veil, apron, long blue skirt swirling. One arm grabbed William Netson. The other swung, hand flattened in a paddle. Her round face stiff. White. She bit her lips. Beat his rear end.
Her hand pulling back, beating down, pulling back, beating down, crucifix around her neck swinging, back, beating down.

Kids on the playground stopped and stared.

William Netson bawled; his face burned red.
He punched back at Sister Beatrice, not about to give up.
He punched at the air.

Lip bleeding, she held him by the shirt collar.
Dragged him along the blacktop.

William Netson. Thrashing. Kicking. Screaming.
The heels of his black shoes scuffing.
All the way across the playground.

She was the smallest, shortest nun.

The gate clanked against the chain link.

William Netson sank heavy.

She picked him up, lifted him up, under his arms.

Kids in line for the bathroom moved out of the way.

Sister Ima came running down the steps of the little school.
A worried look on her face.

Taking one arm.
Sister Beatrice the other.
William Netson. They carried him up the stairs.

Heat rose off the blacktop. I could feel it between my knees. Blue sky, a blanket overhead. Everyone standing around like white marble statues inside the doors at church. With their eyes forever open, looking back at you. Hearing, seeing everything, but saying nothing. No matter where you stand, in front of them, off to one side, in any direction they can see.

This is what it looks like.

Standing in the middle of the playground.

Soft wind swept my hair.
I looked up and saw a butterfly. It was there in the air above the playground. It was a cabbage butterfly, the kind with white wings.

It fluttered like a star.

Jennifer Loftus didn't see it. Her back was turned to it; she was crying and hiding her face in her hands.
I watched it come closer, hover around her shoulders.
It wasn't rare and beautiful like a monarch butterfly. It didn't have wings like stained glass windows. It wasn't striped like a tiger swallowtail, which I have never seen.
It was going to land on her like she was a flower.
I wished it would land on me.
The back of my neck tingled and I shivered; Jennifer Loftus picked up her face. The butterfly flitted away.
"What is it? What is it?" She asked looking over to me, her eyes wide. She couldn't move, afraid to turn around and look.
"It's a butterfly." I said watching it fly.

Higher out of reach.

"It won't hurt you." I said. "Butterflies don't sting."

I wished it would come back and land on me but the white wings fluttered up and fluttered down and floated across the playground. The butterfly. It was lost, looking for flowers. But there weren't any on the playground. Only black asphalt. Wandering from kid to kid, hovering above their heads. They woke up from standing still. Started to move. They went back to playing like before. The butterfly. It was an angel. Heading towards the gate. Along the path William Netson was pulled. Slipping through the chain link. I stared after it, waiting to see it turn and fly up the front steps and inside the little school. Chase after him. Make sure he was okay too. But it didn't. The butterfly didn't do that at all. It kept flying straight ahead into a field of green grass and yellow dandelions.

Sister Beatrice blew the whistle.
Her round face stiff. White.

Kids closest to the gate were first to get in line.

I stood in the middle.

No one said anything.

I wondered about William Netson. If he was okay. If his mouth got washed out with pink powder soap.

It wasn't like he didn't do anything.

He said a bad word.

I knew it was a bad word and I knew I wasn't supposed to say it. I knew I wasn't supposed to talk that way. My mother said it was disrespectful. My father said he'd pound the living daylights out of me, if he ever heard me talk that way, like a gutter tramp.

My father said that word. He said that word and worse, all

the time, and nothing ever happened to him. What would Sister Beatrice do if she heard him, if she heard my father swear?

Kids got spankings when they got in trouble.
By their parents.
I didn't know nuns were allowed.
They weren't allowed. Were they?

Her hand pulling back, beating down.
Third graders stood closest to the gate.
A line for the boys.
A line for the girls.

They stood up straight and tall with their arms at their sides, looking beyond the chain link fence. It was like they practiced walking around balancing Bibles.

Second graders were next, first graders last.

The sun beat down.

Hot.

Standing in silence.

From one to another.

Her eyes moved.

Rested on my shoulders.

She was the smallest, shortest nun.

A trickle of sweat ran under my arm.

Sister Beatrice taught third grade.

All I could think about.

William Netson. Thrashing. Kicking. Screaming.

The sweat under my blouse, under my red sweater.

All the nuns dressed the same. Wore the same clothes day after day. All day long, all year round, even in summertime. That's why, my mother said, it's called a habit. Skirts falling down around the ankles. Long sleeve shirts buttoning up over white turtleneck collars. Black aprons. Black veils. Crucifix on a leather string.

Around her neck, swinging.

Sister Beatrice taught third grade.

I was in second grade.

Turning, she swung open the gate.

Next year.

She would be my teacher.

BLURRED VISION

"I've got to get out. Everyone here is wrapped up in their own little world, with their own stupid problems—and it all means nothing."

He stood in the middle of the room. He was dancing, really, in the center of a crowd. No.

He was there anyways. He was at all the 'gatherings,' wherever they happened to be. I never knew how he managed to be there. He must have known someone. But I never saw him talk to anyone. He just stood there, in the corner of the room. No, he sat on the couch, staring at the lamp. His face, his chin, pointing upwards, bathing under a shower of light.

I was leaning over the kitchen sink, over the dishes and the smell of rot, and someone reminded me of something I once said.

"You said you would never drink."

"Really?"

I was leaning over the kitchen sink, filling a pitcher. Making the mix. The forty-pounder was still in a paper bag and on the counter.

"Who would say a thing like that?"

Nights started like this: at someone's house. My house maybe. In the living-rooms and bedrooms. The bathrooms. It was all the same. People would drink and talk. Idle, really. Then, we'd leave half-cut for an intended destination. So-and-so was spinning there. DJ whoever was in town. Or sometimes it was just a frequented bar, a place we went to on any given night, if nothing else was going down. Afterwards, there were these 'gatherings.'

When I opened my eyes, I didn't remember where I was, or what I was doing. I looked across the table and my girlfriend looked away. Some guy had his arms around me.

That's when I felt it coming. I stood up and tried to hurry to the bathroom. I made it a few steps, slammed into the wall, and threw up. Then, I leaned forward to catch my breath. I rested my arms on my knees. In another setting, I might have been a runner after a close race. My girlfriend came over and gaped at the floor. The vomit was mostly clear, but had green chunks floating in it. She broke the silence with a laugh and slapped my butt. "I don't even remember you eating," she said.

He seemed like everyone else. He wore long, kind of baggy
cords, low, almost below his buttocks. His boxers were higher, around his
waist.

He walked as though he had nowhere in particular to go. He had a beer
in his right hand, and a smoke tucked behind his ear. His shoulders
rocked to the music.

But he wasn't like everyone else. I can't quite put my finger on it. Maybe
it was because he never said anything, really. He would move closer to his
side of the couch when a host came around. He never put his tongue out
to receive. He never did what was cut on the table.

He never stumbled. He never sputtered. He never said anything, really.
He wore glasses with thick dark rims. I don't think he needed them.
He seemed to see just fine.

I went to sit beside him and felt the couch shift as I did. My house was
having a party, and I told him to come.

They were bleeding ulcers, the doctor explained. I was too young to have ulcers.

Did I have a lot of stress in my life? she asked. I laughed. I was too young to have stress.

Well, did I drink a lot of alcohol? she enquired. Again, I laughed. How did she suggest I avoid having stress?

When I danced, it didn't matter. It began that way, and it would never change. Sure, I was watched, but for the first time in my life, maybe, I didn't care. No one did. Maybe that was the drug that started it.

My girlfriend rolled her eyes. She'd heard this all before. She thought it was embarrassing. She started braiding portions of her hair, and looking out on the dance floor.

"Let's go," she said.

In her car, she lit a cigarette. "That shit," she said, "that shit that you always say—is it true?"

It was, I thought.

"I've got the same deal," she said, glancing around at her car.

"Parents, all they do is give you money, and drain you."

At six in the morning, the sun was coming up. I was on the couch, hugging my stomach. There were bottles on the coffee table. Cans on top of the tv, and plastic cups falling over the floor.

A friend of mine came to carry me, like a baby, down the stairs and to my room. It was cooler down there. Outside the windows, I saw the shadows of people's feet. The air was musty; it was always that way. He undressed me and placed me on my bed. He took a shirt from the floor and licked its sleeve. He used it to wipe the dried puke from the corner of my mouth.

Then, he lay down beside me, and put his face in my hair. His leg across my waist. I could feel his eyes, his mouth waiting.

"He didn't come." I announced.

My girlfriend gave me a funny smile. We sat on the porch in our bikinis, drinking beers. Her small breasts rested on her ball-like belly.

"I'm so tired," she said. "I just want to get away."

It was morning. The sun seeped through the airy moisture and was melting away the clouds.

We sucked our beers like nipples, staring at the crimson glare behind our eyelids.

When I woke in the afternoon, the sun was immediate; the world seemed blue through my squinted eyes. But the skin between my breasts was red and filmy.

When I saw him again, he apologized without delay.

"I had to work late," he explained.

I pretended like I didn't care. As if I didn't remember. It made him uncomfortable. He shifted to his other leg.

Meanwhile, I drifted. But, feeling heavy and bloated, I was anchored to the floor. I tried to lean against a table and ended up with my face in someone's lap.

I don't know what happened after that. Maybe I went home. Maybe I slept on the carpet. Maybe I woke the next morning in someone else's bed. It's all the same.

Except, that was the last time I saw him. I mean, I saw him around after that. But I never said anything to him.

Occasionally, I scanned through the crowds, to catch a glimpse. His eyes looked bigger through the windows of his frames. I still see him, every so often in my mind, staring under that lampshade, the skirt of the world.

FLIP AUFOPFERUNG FLY

: an impropoganda
Or How to Become a Caesuricide Squad Wing Commander

Dear language,

As both subject and object of the barbarous atrocities of this world, you have been subordinated, subjected, disciplined into dramatizing, qualifying and parceling the world in adjacent matrices; forced to hierarchize and contain the turbulent fluxes, facts, fractions, fracas of war, power and the control of information. And though you remain as an unflailing witness to these continued atrocities, your witnessing is "a witnessing that is true by a truth irreducible to the truth of disclosure and that recounts nothing that shows itself". (Levinas) And, as this witnessing occurs not in the form of a dialogue but in dysymmetry (in the fundamental inequality of that originary relationship), you inhabit a sybilline space, an aporetic plais of traces, phantoms, specters. Speaking not of the event, but the impossibility of recuperation.

Inscribing a "**POSTHUMOUS INFIDELITY**" (Proust) & stand in for the impossibile adequation—always already represent that excess [excédence] over the present

And, as you erupt into yourself, you are a revolution

dancing warlike—positing yourselves as a hermetic structure—
presenting yr own hermetic lexicon, yet secreting
yr unbalanced systems. And, even as you are "bootwhipped into
plump union", mobilizing your forces and articulating your damage,
how i admire you,
yr radical abscess—

overflowing on the front lines
on the outskirts of an utterance,
in the phrasal interface of
enfolding inflexions

And, in this excess of engagement,
you represent an intertextual matrix of dissidence, resistances,
lineages, histories, bloodlines, connexions. i don't even know who you
are anymore. disarticulating through vagrancy, abjection—yr very
presence implies a web of conspiracy and underground operations.
Indwelling you inhabit a labyrinthian space of vertiginous networks
that emerge in the site of its production; create yourself in the process
of habitation. And sometimes, you go "underground". i don't know
where to find you.

We're going on a b   hunt.
We're going to catch a big one.
What a beautiful day!
We're not scared.

Oh-oh! A cave!
A narrow, gloomy cave.
We can't go over it.
We can't go under it.

Oh, no!
We've got to go through it!

And when i do—you are mangled and bleeding. Have become
distorted systems, antimonies blown to bits. Yr meaning gets
hijacked—taken up, transported to unknown destinations.
It never arrives.

"the pilot of the little airplane had forgotten to notify the airport of his approach" (Hejinian, My Life)

Zaum. Zaum. Zaum.

" . . . a plane of consistency of multiplicities, even though the dimensions of this plane increase with the number of connections that are made on it. Multiplicities are defined by the outside: by the abstract line, the line of flight or deterritorialization according to which they change in nature and connect with other multiplicities. The plane of consistency (grid) is the outside of all multiplicities. The line of flight marks: the reality of a finite number of dimensions that the multiplicity effectively fills; the impossibility of a supplementary dimension, unless the multiplicity is transformed by the line of flight; the possibility and necessity of flattening all of the multiplicities on a single plane of consistency or exteriority, regardless of their number of dimensions . . ." (Deleuze and Guattari)

And, as you take me (with you)
in a Cixouvian or Bernsteinian "withness" (a relational witness)
or a Heideggerian "Being-with"—as you collapse our distance
with "contagious proximity", "negotiated adjacency",
and (L. sui; of oneself cidium; from caedere, to kill) cecidi caesus, to
cut, to pieces,

scindere scidi scissum
abscissa

i am a caesuricide bomber; of ruptures, gas(s)ps, absences
explosions. a tsuriside bomber of psycho-social
upheaval, a sluicide bomber; drenched trough flume floodgate.

as in a conduit that serves to carry off the surplus; as in "**by this
fresh blood that from thy manly breast I
cowardly sluiced out**".
a Seusside bomber

I will balm them here or there!
I will balm them anywhere!
In a car. In a bar.
In a bus. What's the fuss?
I will balm them in a hall.
I will balm them in a mall.
I will balm them as we drill.
I will balm them, yes I
will.

biddy biddy bombe' of permutation, modulation, reverberation
ciphered alliances where meaning is cut off / out / into

a circumcised language, i
cirquemcize language, fold in
on as wounds, words. Cut into
& fly

'cause when volé is to fly and to steal,
i fly away in you stealing. lift.
off appropriating with exuberance (with terror)
über errance, abberance

And, i am asking: How does one give oneself death
{se donner la mo[ ]t} when putting oneself to death
means dying while assuming responsibility for one's
own death committing suicide but also
sacrificing oneself for another, dying for the other,
thus perhaps giving oneself death, accepting the gift
of death ? How does one give oneself death when
that death is only a representation of it, a figure, a
signification or destination for it? How does one
give it to oneself in the sense of simply, and more
generally, relating to the possibility of death when
that possibility an appearance, a polis, an aporetic
presence, an impropriety in the Heideggerian sense
of propriety, la propre: when to own is to own up to,
to give oneself over to , what then is the relation
between putting oneself to death and dying for
another · when every other is every bit other? What
are the relations among sacrifice, suicide, and the
economy of the gift? the guest to the host or
hostess to ghost list: suicide supplements
symptoms the impossibility of
substitution...

And, if the official meaning of terrorism is *what obstructs official and corporate business* (for example, Canada's Anti-Terrorist Bill, Bills C-35 and C-36) which defines *terrorist as what is intended to cause serious interference with or*

disruption of an essential service facility or system (as evident with Bill C-35 83.01 (1) (B) (II) (E)), i write this infected writing, an entre-fearance of frayed ruptures / of non-systemized facility—a hyper-intentional serial inter-referenced eruption of contingent surfaces

which calls for inscription
of not patriotic events, images, an overpowering
monopoly of meaning
but a fanatic factionalism
of looming accumulates, secretions—
incorporate porting
courting porous topos.
portals

Bomb ditty bomb dirty bomb, bomb, bomb.

SHOEISSANCE.

And, in this non-stop succession of disruption
(which keeps the reader in a continual state of inner anxiety) / as i
give myself over to you, the question to ask is who is
hijacking who? hi jack, it's…What's at stake? Who
is the controlling body? For how long? Whose mission?
Whose alliance? Who has the last word?
What is being articulated? And why?

(((hi jack of all trades)))

an interiorization which questions
a topology of limits

an anti-absorptive non-colonizing aporetic prolixis, which i pass
through; wrinkled, furrowed, folded

And with "the unbearable paradox of fidelity",
my connection to you demands an ingathering

of hijacked ejaculates /

but only by exceeding,
traducing, wounding, injury, traumatizing the very
interiority that you inhabit

And, as Levinas points out "the distancing of the i [draws] me closer to myself discharged of the full weight of my identity", i now live in you. my home, homily, hemorrhaging homonymous, heimish, yet unheimlich,

```
                              in the house that
                              hi jack built
```

with you, in a paratactics of relocations

{{{ like les voiles of the palate,
palette. pilot. pile. pit
plotting postulates

wrested in the micrology of the minor loci of
concurrent logic }}}

which fissures / between coherence and heterogeneity,
between singularity and iterability

And, through a history of secrecy, sublation,
responsibility / rapt
with dysfunctional fusions,
fussy clusters coiled with
economies of sacrifice, i
become you, a visceral production of veils, values, villas, volés,
volleys, turns, tours, tournées, intricacies, versions, conversions,
camouflages, masquings, perversions.

And with every narration, récit,
every confession, every
relation or report (rapport),
i smuggle myself into this unwarranted *wahre* welt,
die warheit / into the knotted estrangement
of plotted pastiche postulates, the
plump suckling
of a glossolalic flailing matrix and

celebrate you, an irrational contagion; with intoxifying proximity.

haibun of the darling foundation

1

Awake / This is This. Scriveners, my eyes draft the dark of a room so vital and lustrous it had never any use for the artificial. Beneath the plaster a crush of wires glimmer in the flash over; air, referring back to sound, cites breathy flickering of newborn organisms, clear and glazing The New Electric Library. I am driven by touch. I get out of my bed and my hand is on pulse and fire. I touch the wall I am pressing my body against the wall there is nothing so warm as here. You are lost and gone forever. The dark room, the light house, the pace of streets receding with such purpose or chance composite. I am as yet held under sky, promise, broken, transcribing a language i have not yet learned to censor. My heart bleeds a subculture of waiting at each busstop, every drop of my barely-here body a transfer of zones. Who blushes even in the presence of architecture. My face succumbs to pink, chimerical skin moving between the corporate, crawling with the blazing ardor of the other in the city of mediocrity, smooth and cool and vicious. These buildings and those plebiscites; all blueprints and fortunes, the farthest reflection of my shaky luminosity. Becoming of ashes, la bruit and a trial of sparkling lies. Look. Love. Dust, red. Dreadful sorry, Clementine. In the trailer it is Mexico and the truck must have gone over my body eleven times to the ethereal exponent. I tell my mother, when I grow up I want hair on my arms as thick and black as the boy's who sheds clothing in the sand by the highway through the heat hazed air

we sleep we don't know why
we translate daytime to our ghostly darlings

2

Each breath is a rare manuscript. How many misprints and minutes struck out to compose the single inhale of now. Fever, mexico, cityscape: rustling like paper dresses behind the retina, each segment of time hooks onto the next, decadent and fierce as an angel's poison. These days I find I cannot write straight lines have taken to ripping paper deconstructed clothing. I sign my name each time in a different tense or a different gender. I cannot wish straight. Watching myself get useful on paper I wonder, with which skill did I pick up these chilling habits. When did I designate certain eyes to be walked like planks, upon whom do i bestow my inhibited similes, truncated heartbeats. I am driven by the visual. In the galaxy I am so small that my body folds easily into the space between the front and back seats complete with room for a teaparty. We are on a journey. Vertical irises carve densely through the feminist politic and usurp my own articulate fingers in plagiarised ceremony to the finite frame: page. We sense a room of people, empty save for sparse greys and greens and the smell of hospital cleanliness, where mouths open full of voice and saviours. It is of course the kundalini running rampant from tailbone to ether. I quickly assign my raggedy dolls like missiles to the darling foundation of an arsenic lifeline. You can see my hand now rising from behind the chair and you laugh for it is inside the felt of a homemade puppet. You sit back. Sigh and release. At last, you are about to experience a spectacle from the skeletal

curiously, my pen is found to have no reproductive organs

3

Les contes de fées, waterbabies, saltimbanques. Anastasia, how pretty do we name our ugly sisters. cut are darling dynasties from the close lyric bias of an accident prone preciousness. tongue, wrist, hazard, sing for us our story. beneath the water my feet and around my feet fish of so many horizons and colours they seem able to breed a palette of fantastic sea. I meet here a wave so arrogant she looms all the way from mexico to oregon until choosing me child bride. her lick is voracious it swallows me blue i am high tide. now   I will live with the mermaids. it is here i realize all the words have been replaced with physical symbols, taped slipshod to a crumbling page: they are untranslatable and clarity awaits. Raw and abashed, i turn to hold the paper up as a drawing for it cannot be said. liar, your dynasty is wallpaper, your fleshling watercolour, cut from the lineal. surface: from molecules depth starfish electricity. come breath, abbreviate the air raid, come in gasps of salt and restore my rhythm. Lungs pool their resources to assemble a row of mistaken nouns from the diary of unity: vibrancy, duality, piety. Polarity. here in the backlight of the first survival sits a teenage boy showing photos of persian cats; here my mother washing verbose salt from her only daughter's hair. If structure is important semantics are deadly: a deduction of the fractured and terrific. a person lacking gills is washed up today stiff with adventure and drenched in sea spit. we are told the story of our underwater history because it has no conclusion

blue navigators
     seek out glamorous species
(my life and my bride)

4

Count me this: how many moments lost between now and the time i could have said what i need to say. darling is a tale so discreet and lovely it brings the interrogating voice to its knees, makes coarse the antagonizing of sterile veracity. it is chilled preservation in the mirror stage of itself. cold as pretty, a belligerent beehive   to know your face in the moment life flickers just enough light across it to reveal the masterpiece left by the ambitious athleticism of a five finger hand. subject of pupils, dilation my sweet. to focus the singular means dawning the fetish, material acquaintance   rephrase   a girl in the foreign memorizing for the first time a complexity of red shoelaces, rivets and punctures, the dressing of feet. it takes two women in white to weave a needle as long as an undone dandelion crown once through each of my ears. excellence turns inflammatory and graceless. two holes make a minute. and her shoes were number nine. behind the other wall, the one you have turned and turn to, are the sensual bodies which press together hot with dancing and want of the stranger. here are five and they are alive with nifty taboo: i am slender and glisten in the all-clear. choose one to play for we know your name and we sing it together now in accent aigu. we say welcome, to the residual locale of graffiti read in braille, in complaisance and caffeine and morningtime. city, you cite vague fragments of logos washed up in a bottle, washed by chance to the ocean you sleep by. you shimmer of such profligate angels in the delta rains that you cannot hear even the sound of your plural voice in the breaking news: staccato pawprints seized on sight from a dark gravel road lead to the foundation of contortionists and candy butchers. limbs are only another way of life

sing and be sweet: the
                             new heart breaks fatidic, shards
                                                      the loved one's laughter

5
The tangerine of malignant authenticity rushed and swelling on a clementine bough.
mexico is burning at 6

oh my darling o h
my darling all y ou dar ling s
o my darlingsa ll

6
Overgrown now in numbers, secrets, 6 of age and witness to the hot spell: I of an anarchist beauty once spelled clear and fanatic in wristbone now bound. out of time

and candour i creep to knowledge opening palms and lips
of partial shadow, penumbra. i am driven by

precision. in bed and sentience the fever awakes words, perfect
footprints at the very edges of a sheet of paper.
procedural limbs making vice versa

to shy nowhere and then. clementine. leafing unbridal and vulpine
through woods in the presence of water. teeth

smiling a century of cool grass urbanity, savage
fancy, the familial metonymy. mother. is blindfolded, is swinging

a dead branch to proliferate the treasurefold: jewels tumble saccharine
from a confetti donkey, splaying the ground be'wilded and merciless
to form. i see

the legacy. vivid, exclamatory, rushing to fancy, my feet so
annotate the scalding sand, mischief so lightning my eyes, the dying
day and

so all the night-tide i lay down by the side
of my darling my darling my life and my bride

in the sepulchre
there by the sea in her tomb
by the sounding sea

Holoforms.
Holoforms.

take heede on't make it darling like your precious eye
a man wondering in gait or dazed in appearance is said to be

suffering from darling pea
commonly used as a term of endearing address

little cyclops
my defying is to me

six and darlings all, the
missing princes

the red country
answer, darling, answer, no

a favourite, a minion
deor

DUST
DUST

8

*W*ake derelynges of fever   (dialating   visionary

sicilyshows   a room of mosaics and white linen tremors
dark a young man before the bed clothed
of suspendersgreensoiledpants the fibre of a t hin shirt that has
seen   and turned away
my grandfather. look. his face. concerned. tenebrous. vernacular.

          eyess peak al one int he oldcountry outlining
     ghostlygesture against en chanted

                              morning

                                   displaced

                         ances

                              tress, what do
you do. (I am foreign to this extreme heat i burnup sift like a spirit through
                    these hottrances

one step back and all-clear   in insitence   darling darling of darlingofthepeople
youth skinning tumescent the juice of apple the hybrid of sour-orange
tangerine the factor of 6
a calculated shedding of the clairvoyant child   re member

                                   inamorata, underline

                                   beloved

cyclonic winds   *crinum flaccidum*   darlinglily   *here come the dead*

JUNK MAN'S DAUGHTER

NOT IT
for Lois, vanished

that night
was it cream you wore or white
late eighties' fashion
red plastic bangles
clinking as you danced

next day, in our car passing
we wondered
why you still had not opened
the sign in your window
closed

it took twenty-four-hours to believe
you were missing
and by then you must have been
twenty-four-hours away
in some basement, on some road

since then, mom's concluded:

> your webbed toes are a Godsend
> the middle ones, the two you tried to sever
> as a girl, butter knife clenched in your childish fist

how we'll identify her, there will be no mix-ups,
the toes will tell us, prove all

on more hopeful days, she asks:

do you think she's eating all right?
I wonder, is she still keeping her hair that funny blonde?

in a field searching
surrounded by wood
the whole world
has become a hiding place

counting to ten
a game of hide and seek
I want to bring you racing
towards the trees
your lungs heaving between each
not it, not it

the police say *please, quiet, let's be realistic, dear.*

and the newspaper reports:
   the newspaper reports:

after dance / community
apartment / alone
cup of tea / the kettle / electric
boiling / pink housecoat
bed / turned down
clue / less than

night, and I imagine you sliding your garments, down
step away, your toes curl, fluff the front of your hair, so like you
it is clear, you were alive

death comes creeping from
maybe a closet, a door
stumbling like a drunkard
death, death undresses itself in the dark

DRINK YOUR MILK

eventually. he stopped
lifting his head
opening his beak and feasting

the yolk we fed
ran down his neck
dried sticky on your fingers
his delicate down lacquered, stiff
the dropper flooding his body

you would not stop
he was yours first, so I let you
lift him from the box filled
with grass and rock
the formula we used for every captive
                    because all animals eat grass
                    find their homes in stone

*

mom washing the kitchen floor
on her hands and knees, humming
(smells like a swimming pool)
she will not look up, submerged until
we ask her to

I am prepared for anything

this:

            oh, for god sakes, get that bird out of here
            it's dead. already dead

and for what comes next

you: it's not my fault.
with the hands that once cupped like a nest
whipped its body against the cupboard door

*

cold   even in the sun
where I place the baby to roast, where flies dance
switch partners, to and fro
until the neighbour cat comes calling
rolling the bird once, twice
as though to say, *you dead?*
or what?

that night quiet   except
be good. drink your milk

BIKE

1

the night before last, he said
    saturday morning.

this means: saturday morning you will get a new bike.

last night, dad said *tomorrow will be your lucky day.*

a brand new bike.

2

    on sunday dad wears his good coat
    oval patches on the elbows
    the Lord is with you (shake hands, say peace)
    and also with you.
    please, send me a new bike. I love You.

3

today is the day because my stomach is sick; mom says *take her.* we
drive past the stores, past the town sign, we cross the white line and go
around cars. *bluehair,* he says *them damn seniors should be shot.* then,
the orchards, trees—pointing in all directions—
I can tell they are lost (keep your windows rolled-up)
then, he says *I know a good place.* the gas station sells ice and bait,
bikes too. *out of the car.*

4

I am standing in the back of a white cargo van
spotted with scabs of rust
seven bicycles leaning
handlebars caught in spokes, tape hanging in ringlets
careful when I turn, so my t-shirt
is not snagged by the teeth of ring, soiled by the grease of chain

      outside, procession of discarded goods
      a pop can rolls, sheets of newspaper flutter by
      like empty wings, past the feet of my father
      and the station men who stand in a circle
      the black in their styrofoam cups steaming

      through tinted windows, the lot looks the colour of sleep

      a piece of foolscap paper, black ink, block letters
      "pay ten and choose one, pay twenty, take three"
      at the top: "BUY-CYCLES"

                      take your time.

5

(bike
      say something
              to me)

I press a spongy seat which looks
like the head of large black dog

hot?, dad asks.

(no, I think.)

hot?

        you know, s - t - o - l - e - n.

(stupid, stupid.)

I flick, with the tip of tongue, my latest loose tooth
it clicks inside my head
when it falls, I'll get a nickel.

6

when we get home, dad says *pop the trunk*
out comes bike
next, a towel and he polishes the frame fast, as though it were a shoe
rips tape with teeth and patches the seat,
        now, go play.
        what's the matter with you? hurry up. hop on.

        on the bike, riding towards Robbie's
        knockknockringring—can Robbie come out to play?

        today is
        your lucky day.

        Robbie has paper money
        and he gives me a shiny silver
        I double him; he is always the same
        ketchup chips and an orange pop, please.
        his fingers stained, pink-red
        an orange moustache that stays with him overnight

Robbie lives with his mother because his dad ran away
the same as my cat.

7

double-back
            Robbie sits, his legs swinging, his shoes scuff the road
                                                this bike sure is noisy.

I stand, legs pumping, my muscles flexing with each push

   Robbie grabs my waist, he thinks he might fall,

the whole ride is squeak until   stop   the chain hangs like a broken
jaw

   we walk home, Robbie whining: *wait-up, wait-for-me*

I walk faster, gripping the bars, rushing towards, away from   something

DON'T GIVE A RAT'S ASS

*   after years of rattling the rat has managed
to chew his way and leave behind his stinking sawdust corner
—a day of wearing the wire snap
didn't quite crack his back as the package promised—

when I entered the pantry and flicked the switch

that sudden light, it had him dancing
head hammering, trap clacking against the tiled floor

and well, he's dead now

*   all this effort, it got me thinking

about the woman I live with and our fighting, say,
over a spot on the dirty brown couch

and the kitchen floor (you try walking to the fridge),
socks sticking like a fly-tape tongue collecting hair, honey,
crumbs from the bread we break

whose turn is it?
(you change that friggin' ashtray)

and do I smell a rat? you bet.

have we started sinking, yet?

*   then yesterday, a chickadee, flirting with his little friend
chicka-dee-dee came, dinged the picture window

his beak splintered like a green branch torn from a tree
and see, there's his smudge across the pane of glass

you can still see it through our prints

and, well, so what?

*   a dying bird blinking at the base of our backyard window
means life. why? because I said so.

BODY AND BLOOD

not sure if you're still alive, but willing yourself to feel as though,
    you slip from the clinic.
behind you, the receptionist is still snug
    in her glass case, restful as a mummy. the doctor is working on
another body now. his nurse, so conscientious, cleans the mess.

*

red, yellow – you are waiting for the light to change – green
    pixels illuminate *man in his own image*. in other words: WALK.

a late-comer speeds around the corner, smell that burning rubber
    giver' gunner, they'd squeal –
                    where you grew up – like pigs

GO, heel hits street, sharp cry and flap of scavenger overhead
    bounce of hammer on nail, echo, escaping the nearby
construction site. you've been told – *in this city, there are two seasons:
winter and construction.*
        crew boys in their faded jeans spit and nod
        you expect at least one to be chewing a long blade of grass

your white shirt sticking to skin – binding – the mixing of flour and
water
    WALK. the orange hand urging, throbbing like a fresh burn – *hurry
up, please* – proceed
your arms swinging against hips, rubbing your wrists raw
you count each step as if it were your last: *This is my body. This is my blood.*
the voice in your head – yours, not yours – shrill as the eyes of a bird
    come home to find her emptied nest:
                      To be given up for you.

sitting curb side, a woman swollen as a puffball – her skirt fanned
   her palms cupped to her mouth
she is threatening to blow a handful of her spores your way
   impregnate you with the stink of unwashed parts

you are convinced; it must still be inside of you.
   a scratching. that sound: when your mother showed you
how to hollow pumpkin with a spoon.
   the rounded lip scraping pulp; freeing seed.

Who is it? – you call and answer – *It's me.*
   Who is it? – you ask – *To whom do you belong?*

standing in the crowded subway car – going home –
   holding your breath as the man beside you leans hard, the lump in
his pants
sniffing like a nose is inconsequential:

                    Where are you body? Where are you blood?

SOUP ALONE

*

spokes in the wheel, broken

the neighbours don't seem to notice
(not like I hear it)
        the squeaking of the stroller as I push along the streets.

    Your baby, my, she is beautiful, but

        don't you think she might be cold?

I pull up my hood, yank the drawstrings tight.
(Inside, I am a living shadow.)

*

in the kitchen, I open a tin,

    eat soup alone (it will not do)
        after every swallow, I repeat his name.

please, understand the rules:

        how to eat soup properly

        (spoon away from yourself
        not towards)

        how to cook meat properly.

if you look through the greasy oven window,
you'll see a broiling duck stuffed with bread and thyme.

I monitor like a mother should (I do)

                                    her five-pound baby,

the roasting pan, a sturdy incubator.

                        and who, you ask, who do I expect?

*

because I wound up making myself over
                        into one-big-mistake
                                    is that why he left?

me, with a baby bouncing in her crib.

because mary k. couldn't do a thing,
my skin orange with foundation.
                        meanwhile, he renovated my insides

changed; a dilapidated house.

yet, I'm still accounted for: *head and shoulders, knees and toes, knees and toes . . .*

                        eyes, ears, mouth and nose

*

upstairs, the baby is upstairs

and this is what I would say (if only he would answer the phone)

listen, I've eaten two blueberry yogourt today, the laundry is drying on
the line

           the baby is on our bed

           why won't he just come home?

cry baby, cry baby I could tell him   *it cries, our baby. it cries,*   I
would say.

my finger pointing at

           her face, hot, a blister ready to burst

           I'd tell him, I can't make her stop

                      not alone.

*

look what I've gone, done:

her hands jutting from beneath the pillow, clenched like pincers; skin
the shade of lobster-blue.

*

soup alone,
>   never seems enough.

and who's left? (will you sit with me at this table?)

>   husband left for a better woman
>   now he eats her cooking, cleans her bones

>   not
>   >   the butcher, the baker, the candlestick maker

>   even you can't say it:
>   >   *caution, that one is best left alone.*

SALTATIONS

A History of Blood

1.

I am looking for a rhythm, a thread
passing through one heartbeat
and out another, a constant motion
weaving pages, stories
binding stories

—this is the journey of my blood.

Birth dates, death dates,
a hyphen resting in-between
(a drawn eyelid), a crease
in history

(The salt doll is 100 years of tears
evaporated, preserver of secrets.
*   She travels with blood,*
mother to daughter gathering
ages, prayers, flower petals
*   press them gently—*

Turning pages, I am turning soil
not for the sake of earth
but to find some hidden treasure

in these black lines, pressed
onto paper, letters
bending into words, whispering
a face, a name

She is the taste of oceans crossed,
    breath that carries.
She holds rising steam of tea and sweat,
    childbirth on her skin.

History of blood is revealed in halves:
half-breed, half-blood, half-truth, I am left
with only half story
the unnamed, the unspoken:
A Cree Woman

Five generations steeped into one small statue
she is history boiled
to solid brine.)

2.

Confessions of a daughter signed in script:
"I, Flora Bell, am a half-breed, head of my family"

blood rushes

Pull history from veins,
learn the equation
of mixed blood.

I am looking for the history of blood
in the face of my grandmother's
salt doll, my inheritance: infinite grains
poured into a skirt, an apron...

I hold her lightly
for fear she'll lose her shape, spill white
between my fingers.

*

Tongue tip to her face—taste
the salt and dust of tears

silence   shifting

Saltations

1. Inheritances

Where salt has eroded her: pores.
The skin of my salt doll, an ivory paste,
flour stirred with rain.

   (Careful not to drop her,

Berry lips, rasped and cracked,
her braids, feathers
curved in memory
of flight.

   she is only weight in my hands

2. Listening with palms

This line, a skin we share.

Grandmother, I wear you
a crease, thumb to wrist.

Everything I have seen
pleated in my palm, the rim of your skirt, a lifeline,
full as a bell.

Where we have grown: silver thread,
stretching

(seamless

3. Taste her

Forehead sweat
in rain. Watch her dissolve
grain   by grain

shoulders   neck   eyes

opaque and
leaching in lines.

Shape lost
like the peal of your name in my mouth
before I learned you

Flora   *Flora*   *Flora*—

Bell

Four Days

Thigh-clenched fistfuls of flaming
moss, the heavy drench
of shame.

What you leave in the woods is a kill site, fustic
blood. At the base of a smoke tree, jaundice root,
a rose petal, rust snow.

Palms open the wound
you carry and the weight
is nothing compared to hunger
staved, or silence.

Red holes in the snow
all the way home.

Arrows.

Nestichio's Story

i.
You are daughter of your father son of father son
of father. Six-years-old, salt-skinned and suspicious
in feathers when you are found and rescued, found
and fathered, found and stolen and lost and
married, 12-years-old who stole
who?

ii.
StoneMaidenCreeMaidenIndianMaidenMother

Bloodlock. Wedlock. Out of
everything, duty.

Stored and folded *stories inside*
stories linen and scarves *hairlocks and*
feathers withered aprons *abdomens* pressed
gloves *fists* broken heels *running,*
running bear cubs, blind
milk-lit *nights* forced to *forced to*
suckle them.

iii.
Salt-scrubbed tongue learning
the speed of blood.

Stranger

I will come to you like an afternoon star, faint
as a lover slipped into the back pew, fall
inside the cathedral of your eye and feign
the quickening of your heart
like snow in lamplight, I will mime
the vowel of your mouth in psalm, take
desire like the scratch of your nail over
and over, a skipped record that keeps you
from remembering
the next word.

(s m i l e)

The silence around
your mouth, laugh lines
I will inherit, the whispered language
of parenthesis, an inside cue
to smile (now) pose the appropriate
question (a drink?) to know the precise
pressure a cold cloth relieves
from his (drunken) head, the mists
of perfume it takes to conceal (a lover's)
desire, the perfect temperature
to burn the breakfast (ever-so)
slightly, when to leave
a faint smoke
on the tongue.

Highway Recitations (you learn going home)

i.
the distance:
wing-trimmed sky
       falling behind
       in grey
              clippings

distal rain—
veins
       and veins

back of hand spitting blue

this land, a wrist bone
pulsing sky

ii.
Vista Nursing Home

I am seeing you seeing
me awkward, pale-
skinned and hungry when you ask:
when am I going home?

iii.
highway recitations:
Grandpa's deer whistles streaming sky,
all the way home a shrill cry

sing it:
....
iiiiiiiiiiiiiiiiiiiiiiiiiiiiiiiiiiiiiiiiiiiiiiiiiiii

iv.
trying to hold on to myself because it's all I've got to show you

v.
small talk
driving past the flood along sky-bruised land
is this what Kerouac meant when he said he could see
through the earth?

vi.
power lines losing ground,
river rising, swollen fields,
a necklace of crucifixions

vii.
what you miss the most is listening to wings thrumming at the feeder

we talk holding hands, humming
in your bones, birds
willing flight

viii.
tulips
ripe yellow,
petals cupping rain

      —what you saw the last time you lived April

now only acrid air,
flowers choking you

like the candy you swallowed
when you heard his body, fall
water-heavy, fail   *take those flowers away*

ix.
if only we could see the entire road from here:
pendants of frozen teardrop steeples, cloud
blue, the color of air

x.
wings of morning light, branch-hatched sky
when you close your eyes
what is the first color?

xi.
fill your palms with sky-belly, watch
your knuckles curve the land

Moth Lake, Fishing Album
for Great-Grandpa D.

Dusk

> Bass in your hands is a limp lung sighing, gills loosen
> lichen strands, thin pellucid mouth.
>
> Hook dropped only a foot
> and I know you can't see how far my line goes
> below the surface. Disappointment is your rod bending
> a tight line, torn spine.

Rescue

> Pickerel on the dock (not breathing but eyes alive, scales
> and scales of green sky) Grandpa at the gutting block, my foot
> curving fish belly, white on white, cool mushroom-
> skinned fish slipped to the edge of
> the edge, gills—

Dragged by the mouth

> a fighting muscle
> *how do you know it doesn't hurt?*
> hook-ripped lip
> *how can you know scales torn from cheeks, or hook*
> *piercing mouth and eye?*

What the fish gills sing

> fish death is what the eyes eclipse what the body,
> *the softness of a sleeping hand*, what the gills, *a hand*
> *inside music*, what the mouth, *shredded tongues*, what
> the scales *filled with sky*, filled
> with sky

and when you slip from my hand what piece of lake
on the dock left, what hole in the water
what shifting

Loose photo/1

in your hand, fish stomach and tired waves
beautiful mouth, slack agape sky
beautiful fin, a feather

Loose photo/2

pike hung at the gill cleft, clear lake fins and
your hands the same limpid ghosts, eyes
the dark center of blood, scent of tin

Loose photo/3

pointing to a loon family, your palm draws
dusk, water-smooth neck, a throat call-
for a moment you have forgotten

Loose photo/4

jack snagged with green jelly lure and beside you
a pale girl prays through teeth for all the fish to
swim, to swim

Blueberry Pie
(from the unwritten recipes)

Pastry

spin & score, spin & score
a giant petal, flour-white, dimpled
berry drum rolling
one   by one, tones
of blue, whole notes
indigo to azure
spoonfuls of rolling skies

Filling

berry pulp loosens seed, a lake
settles, beetles scribble-dance water notes
all afternoon, sun lengthens
berry stems, pulled by the thirst
of petals

Timing (one song, danced)

this is where you begin: vinyl drips
syrup-slow air, a slack dust-

twirl, storms
echo the roots of your hair
backlit

over   & over,
the needle bleeds Billie, *Long Gone*

hips reel his hand to your weight-
less,   water languid
limbs, arms sway
the timing of waves

purple finger-
tips, lips blue-stained
syncopated kisses, random

perfections of a pebble-
ellipsed shore

Not Confession

This is not to confess, but to apologize for that car ride after
berry-picking, the day I tipped a full bucket over my stubborn head,
purple-thumbed locked grandpa's keys in the trunk, swigged back the
last of the orange crush in the backseat vinyl-stick '76 Olds, berries
jiggling my teeth, fingers stained blue your peach scarf on my head
like a sunset, *Grandma, grandma grandma I want to swim! jump! splash
so big my waves will tip a whole family of loons.*

That day in the middle of my own lake, the only day you ever tossed
words over me, a steady current of berries, blue
ripe-skinned tears.

NUTMEG MEWS

0. Earl's

So there i am sitting in earl's with my friend leila telling her some kind
of story or maybe not maybe what i'm doing is something more like
taking out a little package we both do this a lot and placing it on the
table maybe we're talking about violence again not so much violence
against women as violence and women or for that matter violence and
children and who knows what it is really oh yeah i understand violence
oh yeah you remember the time mickey's head the black cat the nights
in the closet and she's answering oh yeah the baseball bat and it's like we
just kind of turn the package over in our hands

///to admire the wrap the shine of the paper the accomplished
precision of the bow but we never open it not anymore never get
beyond that we could if we wanted to open sesame moment with its
magic words oh yeah that's what opens the door oh yeah oh yeah we
acknowledge with our eyes our hungry looks knowing this time for
sure the wrapping the little special twist our tone can give the bow the
edge of the hidden words is worth so much more to us than the
contents more pleasant anyway so leave it there in the middle of the
table the air between us a pretty package wrapped like that open
sesame and turn away

///so maybe the magic in the words is more like a secret password a
sign or countersign *consigna* they say in spanish though that's more a
slogan or maybe it's more a countersigh a long sigh anyway while
we're just kind of looking away from both package and words only

then she laughs laughs and says you could do it that way you know
you could it's possible do your whole life like that all these little stories
we never actually tell after awhile and now we're onto that describing
without ever quite telling them again how these are the ones we just
write headlines for and leave alone make them into the who goes there
who goes there of the middle of the night of our lives the open sesame
of a dark cave we don't want to look into just know who's passing by
just enough to remember ourselves and i just laugh oh yeah oh yeah
that would be good i say really good write them down and then
because i don't know if she means me or some kind of anyyou anyyou
at all i sort of say well one could one could i suppose but i wouldn't i
certainly wouldn't though it's sort of inspiring i tell her one's
autobiography my whole autobiography this life i've been thinking too
much about as headlines

///just make a list and let the reader write the story what a novel way
of dealing with the novel or even the memoir i say and besides what a
great way to get out of this constant pondering to escape trying to look
at the questions contained behind the words to never resolve anything
and i'm even starting to like it when she says oh no not at all you have
to actually do it write them down first the headline then the whole
story the story to match the headline write the whole thing all the
details gory or not remember the headline then write the story one two
three four and she counts with her fingers beginning to end and i say
yeah right yeah right then oh no

///oh no no way and just laugh again not me not me and besides i
couldn't i really couldn't you don't understand i say i couldn't

///and by then it's true and that's what's strange maybe a moment
before it wasn't but the minute i say it it's true as if this truth too was
hiding there behind the headlines the pass words the countersighs
because no matter how much i try to hide behind that pretty
packaging the minute i i think about doing it actually telling all these
stories this is what happens all the stories are gone there are no stories

left behind the headlines what were those stories anyway i find myself thinking there's nothing inside the package it's not just my laugh that's hollow it's my life like the cave is open the cave is open the open sesame cave that's supposed to contain not that storied treasure but those treasured stories all hidden right inside and instead it's just hollow and echoing and full of stalagmites and tites and things to slip on i can't even see and i've already fallen even in that restaurant back into the darkness and now i know that's what i've been avoiding that's what i've been wrapping in my pretty phrases my bright ribbons of storyless words it's the stories i've forgotten i have no map no x marks the spot for the darkness no longer contains stories or headlines or passwords or anyone who goes there who goes there at all not anyone who can lead me out anyway so i just look up

/// from the table and out to the windows and out the door and try to see it how the sun is still shining the sun is still shining it's the middle of my own bright day and the sun is still shining i haven't opened anything this isn't a cave or the dark inside of an empty package and leila i say leila touching her hand leila i say look out there that's not a headline or a story look out there look out that window you see those leaves you see that sky all that brightness that's my autobiography that's my autobiography out there that's my autobiography you can write that headline if you want the sun still shines it's a great password the leaves are green is the countersign because that's all it's ever been it's all that effort to keep the day bright forget the rest and keep the sun shining that's my autobiography my only autobiography only i can't you see i can't i can't even say it i can't.

1. **Stuck finger blues rrrrrrr rrrrrrrr rrrrrrrr**

Like i said the truth is i don't want to do this at all you know what i mean i'm not the least interested that's what i keep telling myself it's just not where i'm at conversations in restaurants with their little headlines are one thing telling the whole story any whole story something else altogether that's what i think and not for the first time as i sit down at the computer at the computer again always again

///you want a whole story well i'll give you a whole story that's right a whole story maybe i'll just write a novel instead that's right like a real novel you know what i mean storyline and setting and point of view and above all those consistent characters consistently constructed i've done that before or at least i think i have more or less consistent anyway done that always in never out of character thing only even as i think it try to make that plan try to find a story place with a logic of its own lifting my right hand to thumb my very real nose at an imaginary leila i can't i already know i can't

///the stranger truth overcomes the consistent fiction and the inconsistent just ride it out if you can darkness descends so sitting at the computer with my thumb on my nose not even waving is just about all i can manage these days there's no letters on the screen responding to my fingertips it's all i can do to get a pencil a chalk crayon into that hand to make myself draw in fact the only place the sun is shining is out my fingers i can't seem to get the day colours back at all that bright sun i spoke of in the restaurant there's just this thing of sitting in the dark and pouring the only colour in the universe out my fingers like a little light through a crack in the door that i'm slowly opening to see if the coast is clear until there's this one morning i wake up and maybe i'm just too caffeinated from the morning coffee or too hung over from the night before or maybe it's just so very very tired from work or conversations in restaurants i don't want to have but too shaky anyway far too shaky

/// for the discipline of drawing so i figure i'll just do it just do it the way leila said just do it just make my list and begin just begin that's right begin it should be fun i tell myself i need something to do so begin just begin i'm too wired too awake just begin and there's my fingers on the keyboard and doing that thing sort of like a piano player shooting back her cuffs and fingers across the keys letting my

fingers float across the letters asdf gh jkl semi-colon g qwer ty uiop zxcv
bnm comma period back slash

///only that's all that will come out you see no matter what i tell myself
i've got no list no list at all absolutely none not a single one of those
headlines will allow itself back into my mind there's no restaurant and
no sun and no one to finish my sentences or for that matter to begin
them no one no interlocutor but myself and i'm silent i'm hiding in the
dark so it's just the dark just the dark the longest time just the dark
that's all the dark the dark and my fingers moving making nonsense
instead of music or even words asdf qwer ty uiop bnm comma period
only i can't think of anything else to do not even get another coffee so i
just sit there in the dark that isn't dark it's bright out my window and
let it happen asdf gh jkl semi-colon qwer ty uiop z until my index
finger comes again to the r and sticks rrrrrrrrrrrrrrr

///rrrrrrrrrrrr rrrrrrrrrrrrr rrrrrrrrrrrrrr

///and suddenly it's that rrrrrrrrrr rrrrrrrrrrr jiggle jiggle buncha
phoneys buncha phoneys thing mickey always did my mother mickey
and then it's mickey in the cab and this voice saying something and it's
my voice my voice only much younger and you see there it is right
there right there in that voice you've got your first headline in that
voice your first password sign or countersign 26 nutmeg mews my
voice says only it's more than that it always is

///rrrrrrrrrrrr rrrrrrrrrrrrr jiggle jiggle and i'm telling the whole thing
reciting the streets of how to get there that's right how to get back to
26 nutmeg mews telling the driver the way home the way i'm sitting
in the dark and telling myself the way back even if it's not home never
was not a real home really but still it's how to get back through the
dark how to get back rrrrrrrrr rrrrrrrrr rrrrrrrrrr

///and how to get back and how to get back over and over the way it
was over and over that cab ride over and over not last exit but last taxi

to brooklyn that's right to brooklyn brooklyn i tell the guy brooklyn over the bridge the brooklyn bridge and i don't know why i'm doing this at all i just am not the tunnel now the bridge i say and maybe it's that little yellow light on the top of the cab maybe it's like just gleaming in the dark and i have to move toward it you know the one i mean what does it say i can't even remember what it says

///*libre* they say in spanish *libre libre* free free it's an old old joke from my days in mexico you ask the cabby are you free and he gives you that mexico city that new york cabbie look and yes on bail he says and switches off the light as you get in and isn't it strange how i can remember that but not what it says on the top of a cab in english in new york when it's free i know it's not vacancy that's a motel and motels are from a whole other time and place i don't even think they'd invented motels yet when i was getting into that cab with mickey or only just because they were so new no one had stayed in their like before on our one trip back to mickey's home town along for the ride we were with car blessed cousins and a dog that would only pee on the new york times

///vacancy signs by the road remain a country western song a road trip like that one wisconsin june only one i was ever out of the city so this sure isn't country no headlines in my life for country at least not for a long time and no road trips either just cab rides so let's just go back a moment to where that one bright light is because it's the only colour among all the grey shadows the yellow light without any words even that simple *libre* maybe it's just numbers on the signs numbers or nothing maybe it's an absence just a question for wanting to be a millionaire which i always did for getting out of there wanted to win the lottery or some contest which is what it was in the end that scholarship though this question was likely the cheapest the first one right there the way it is at the beginning for sixteen or is it sixteen hundred dollars what does it say on the top of a cab in new york when it's free only i'll just remember

///rrrrrrrrrr rrrrrrrrrr rrrrrrrrrr so no matter what it says i'm not free or for that matter *libre* not at all not with mickey's twisted face grey above me and a new colour now the red slash of her smeared lipstick and pushing her into the cab and rrrrrrrrr rrrrrrrrrr and my own voice repeating the words repeating the streets it's a map now and no one's free no one at all not the cabbie and not me no one's free that's right to brooklyn to brooklyn last taxi to brooklyn because they never want to go to brooklyn they always tell you they can't get back at least not with a fare so i want to tell those cabbies i can't get back either and it isn't fair can't get back or even out there's no exit not first or last just no exit at all from brooklyn not my brooklyn so i just smile instead the way i am right now over the keys my nicest nicest pasted on little kid smile and i say don't worry

///don't worry it's just over the bridge

///don't worry with mickey rrrrrrr rrrrrrrr and trying to hit the cabbie buncha phoneys buncha phoneys whaddaya mean it's too far while i try again it's very close i say very very close i don't want to try to find another last taxi i really don't not me very very close i repeat first exit off the bridge not the tunnel the bridge that's right the brooklyn bridge and talking and talking i finally get her in talking and talking so he doesn't get another chance to say no before i'm in myself and i've closed the door and maybe he feels sorry or maybe he knows it really is close who knows but there we are and rrrrrrrrrrrrrrrr rrrrrrrrrrrrrrrr rrrrrrrrrrrrrrrr

///mickey's snoring or maybe still singing buncha phoneys buncha phoneys and we're on our way he's starting to move no more chance to be told no all i have to pray for now is it's not one of those rides when she pees and not on the new york times all polite like wolf the dog but on the seat like that one time on the subway the seventh avenue express with tim when we had to leave her because she wouldn't get off no matter what we did she wouldn't get off we passed our stop and she wouldn't get off i hardly remember it but tim sure does being the

man of the house at ten instructed to take care of me and mickey too
and to ignore the social worker type who tried to save us as mickey
sang rrrrrrrrr rrrrrrrr rrrrrrrrr while for me it's just a vision of the
puddle looking back from the subway door

///a flaring of the nostrils for every time i stand on the platform of
dekalb station the echo of the smell of alcoholized piss down the years
from elevators and car seats and beds and floors so who really cares if
she pees or not except the cabbie this time the shame will be brief
because the one thing i know is she'll have to get out he'll make sure
she gets out no matter the condition of his cab so this is better
especially since tim isn't here the air is solid with summer heat and tim
is at camp so who cares if she passes out on the front stoop not a stoop
at all really just one stair and the two stones to the sides like railings or
like seats where we will hunker down back to the building legs to the
sun or moon so many days so many nights so what can i say if she
collapses into that hollow before the door except it's better than
holding her up singing on the street so already i feel the relief as the
little light that once said free or whatever it is whatever magic
numbers that light turns off and i'm in the dark with my finger still
stuck rrrrrrrrrr rrrrrrrrrrr rrrrrrrrr

///the rrrrrrrrrrrrrrrrr of the cab and the rrrrrrrrrrr of mickey as it
starts to move rrrrrrrrr rrrrrrrrrrr rrrrrrrrrrrr until my voice resumes

///all over again that's right you got it now over the bridge and the first
exit that's right you take the first exit the first exit not the last exit the
last exit and you've gone too far so first exit to brooklyn the first exit
off the bridge in any case the one to your right then straight through
and a left down henry if you get to hicks it's too far again you'll have
to circle and who wants to do that my best child being grownup voice
my imitation sober mickey hail a cab voice while drunken mickey
keeps it up the rrrrrrrrr rrrrrrrrrrr rrrrrrrrr the stuck finger chorus
rrrrrrrrrrrrr rrrrrrrrrrrrr rrrrrrrrrrrrr

///it's down henry to state and a left on state you can't take jerolemon because it's the wrong way you take jerolemon from clinton when you come up atlantic from the tunnel but the bridge is better it's closer that way though i don't tell him how i love being inside its metal shell passing below the girders and imagining myself in the clouds the bright views of the buildings the water that goes on forever out the narrows and into the ocean so that sometimes i can think i'm free too

///not like the claustrophobic white of the tunnel with its marking for every hundred yards you pass to let you know inch by inch how much closer you are to the end of the ride but either way never free even imagined free for long so just do it who cares which way if you come from the tunnel it's columbia to atlantic a right on atlantic and a left on hicks just one block to state if you go too far you can take clinton but you have to circle clinton to jerolemon jerolemon to state and there are too many circles i've been circling for years so let's keep it clear keep the instructions clear to unstick my finger it's back to the bridge and henry to state then left again on sidney and sidney to nutmeg our own small mews those three houses opposite the school that's right nutmeg mews our own street our nutmeg mews and be careful it's only one block and no you can't come up the other side it's just one way one way to nutmeg mews last taxi first exit first exit to brooklyn clinton to jerolemon henry to state up sidney and only one way only one way only one way only one way one way home only it's a dead end

///a dead end

///one way home and no way out so up nutmeg to opposite the school that's right so i might as well tell it tell it like it is tell it like a headline tell it without words tell it without colours tell it like a long dark taxi ride but tell it tell it tell it dead end last taxi first exit over the bridge clinton to jerolemon jerolemon to state state to sidney sidney to nutmeg

///nutmeg to twenty-six that's right twenty-six old twenty-six we always called it old twenty-six and who cares whether or not the fog of the night or the fog of memory is clearing because here we are and i can see it the old wrought iron door and i'm getting the money out and i'm paying the cab and i'm opening the door hoping mickey will follow and that she'll just get into her bed and go to sleep she won't try to go out or get to the bars but just go to sleep while i stay awake at least until the singing stops the rrrrrrrrrr rrrrrrrrrrr rrrrrrrrrr while my mind tells itself stories the way it does now stories of a brighter future the stories i once followed to leave that place even if i left part of me behind so maybe it's true maybe i can do it maybe since i've done it i can do it again maybe to get out of the dark maybe i just have to say it write my headlines on the paper the way that girl once wrote her future in her head write them down and follow them up and this time when i turn around that last time to give those last instructions maybe i can take them too

///because all you can do from a dead end street is turn around the way i tell the cabbie how half way up the block there's a new street that's right the beginning of livingston where you take a right take a right and just keep going keep going till you see the sign for the bridge that's right the sign for the bridge unstick my fingers qwerty jkl semi-colon and the sign for the bridge nm comma period back slash and just keep writing keep on writing because maybe that's all they are all they've ever been all these headlines are just the instructions for leaving so maybe this time if i just do it i'll get it right not the bridge or the tunnel take the first exit then go across to henry left on henry henry to state left on state to sidney up sidney to nutmeg nutmeg to old twenty-six open the door but just back in the cab back in the cab with all my headlines held in my hand like the new york times and no more mickey to pee on it no more baggage asdf take that one right turn that one right turn uiop and just keep going just keep going watch for the sign the sign for the bridge zxcv let it begin.

NERVE-STORMS

1 *GREEN BENEATH; ECCENTRIC* . . .

campestre: an open field, verdant and brain-rich; a succulent place,
   resplendent with Autumn Joy,
portulaca, *Coryphantha*. your palms prickle confusion and electricity,
   your senses sun-keen, idiopathic,
tongue a ragged burlap of words (bramble, cruciferous, clipped bite of
   mustard).

this is aura preceding storm: vein-lightning and thunder; a shock
   shatters a complexity of sky
and miles and miles of eye-quiet and blue.

and this horizon, scattering, into intricate omen and bone (crossed
   fingers and knuckles
knocked scared, knocked white . . .

2 YELLOW AND FRACTIOUS . . .

bent under fear and the sky (barbed; neuralgic) is hooked with fingers and
    mackerel
(the wind is bristling and you, chattering, all wind-chimes and teeth,
    threadbare nerves).

crossing the nerve-squall is crossing from eye-wall to eye. a surgical edge
intersects your field of vision: below the horizon everything beyond reach,
    and above

brilliant – particles of eye-dust and star, *scotomata*

3 BLACK, MINUSCULE, A MOTE...

wrapped head to foot in shadow. nothing in the air but a slight buzz and
    nothing overhead
but a slow plane, this sluggish sky, a sense of the unexpected. this is a
    dry place, *xerophilus*,
your thoughts tumbling clumps of impulse and tinder: brain-sparks &
    brain-stars.

at night, a diagram of the sky is a detonation staining one side of your
    cerebrum
(the clock counts down meteor showers, hailstorms; small ripples of nerve
    and anxiety).

sleep is a haze that leaves you mind-numb and dank (a blanket of
    fish-scales and sleet,
cold stars glimpsed through the wrong side of a lens)

4 NERVE ENDINGS, REMAINDERS; JAGGED WHITE . . .

neuro-fault line; nerve-quake; *hemicranial*: the wind rips into you—a tree
  split mid-trunk.
this blast is sheet-metal lightning, two plates of a skull pried apart. you
  are frayed optics,
mind a double-edge.

the curve of your sight mimics the night as it surrounds you: dark-domed,
  thick-tongued
drift into sleep (you try to liken this to the embrace of the planetarium
  – you were ten,
and every startling spark erupting in sky or mind, every kern or turn of
  exotic syllable,
held a minute point of departure, a bright speck faraway,

far-off in the future). here, the moon is cut in half . . . no, the whole
  universe is a thought
ruptured
just short of completion . . .

5   *CONSEQUENTIAL GREY; FROST AND ICE; ARBITRARY . . .*

mute and dendritic: November. hoary grey (*incanus*); the river twitching
   with ice and spiders,
long legs and spinning. frenzied. you are tornado-obsessed, thoughts
   wild, whirling,
manic webs frosting your throat.

around you the city is still –glacial & vapour –grey lip of the river an
   undefined syllable: *dri . . . dri . . .*

(water is a pulse that melts the night into harsh beads –stinging throb of
   blood and temple;
inexplicable tears; lacrimation; indispensable rain . . .

6 *INTERLUDE GREY-SCALE; CUMULATIVE; STRESSED MUSIC*
   & WATER-PIXELS . . .

go away, go away. grey is the pitch between bright and brighter.
   half-tones sing nervousness
   (a note stringing well through another month). December, and water an
   approximation
   of colour: collage under white, a sheath of ice over your skin.

you shiver off years' worth of cold, sore bones and teeth (the sky scored
   with scabbard-fish,
silver-white, ice crystals and a frozen lexicon of stars and fragments).
   letters carry little protection;
reading and writing a distraction –of neuron & planet –forestalling
   doom, impending blizzard,
looming ice-fog and sharp shards of apprehension.

rid your arms of cold and ghosts –phantom-grief; rub warmth and
   liniment on your limbs.
memory of pain is a rough incrustation (a scab of storm and foreboding
   –the horizon blood-red,
a line straining your sight); and the blackest sky a soft deception, cotton
   batting drenched
in red. you are caught between seasons; grey sky, white ice,

and the rain, the rain . . .

7 *DYSRHYTHMIC SKY; BLOODSHOT, UNPREDICTABLE . . .*

red red red red red. raspberry (thin vein of blue); tomato (strained through
    yellow). everywhere
red. palms lined with fire & rage, you are fear-marked, brain-scarred,
    your soul choppy with
rough sea and disaster.

angor animi: imminent storm. skies are dangerous (blood draining your
    cheeks) and clouds, menacing
clusters (cumulus congestus), a scarlet band tightening your brow.

the night is spiked with integers: *1 you wake 2 you wake 3 you pace and
    you pace and* . . .
floorboard-weary (flat-footed, languishing pine), you are doubled over,
    tree-green.

*

morning and the sun burns orange in your heart—bile & red sky,
    portentous. in your mouth,
taste of bitter and jagged star; your mind frantic with erratic planets,
    platelets, irregular
orbit

8 HIGH ALTITUDE; THIN, CERULEAN . . .

cacumenus, cauticolis (mountain crest, cliff). roots take hold through the
   top of your head
–*Coryphantha calipensis*, stiff-fingered and needled. you are short of breath
   & balloon-veined, tachycardic . . .

upslope fog. grappling for rope & hook. ascent is a labour of cold words
   and angst.

panting. falling in & out of sleep. falling: over cliff-edge and -hanger,
   body
wrenching   jerking   *myoclonic.* you are wracked with question marks
   and suspense–the forecast low visibility, thick enunciation. ineffable
   lungs.

notes from deep

a single line of lyric on the radio

where are you now?

flood of aching

drench of a woman's voice unseaming me: drift-blue

awash : : the ones who have passed through my body and are lost

awash : : the one who was my body and is lost

                                        where are you now?

what bridge to find you but this   filament of sound this

slenderbow-drawn presence   a hand of piano reaches for

 a voice breaks against

grieving the air bloody

who will do the wide-hipped work of love, her bare-foot walking her voice

egg blue spiking turquoise
the way a march dusk flares

conscious

toward whatever might come
the wrappings of a night not yet known to anyone
dwelling in me tender all the next

day.

now my walking under such a sky
weeping and without an answer for her

but want

of the heart-knot to loosen
where voices reach and cast my days
from a far singing place beyond sense

and want

to go on   recalling how thoughts
seemed to gather in her hands

flight

at her wrists

this verb

happening in the air between us
all through our long conversation

who recall her days   unaccountable

our walking, near   and a child at the hem of the sea, bereft
her sweaty, caught-up gasps and breathing
familiar, arresting us

my wanting the sounds of your thoughts but stooping instead
over her face, the sun rounding her spine, her bend
like a normal curve that means

                                        abandonment. she is

friend deep, my fear, and yours. I see you stand
away, your body's pent, uncried
cry: please don't bring that sorrow here.

only sounds of water touch my skin, the sun,
the child's fractious questions, child I
have no answers for, nor you

except

                I have imagined our mouths discovering each other
                            in talk, words soft as neap-tide melting
                        on shore pebbles at evening, the wash and seep

                                    and hush, I imagined
                                    the fall of our voices
                                    into shadow

        her hands and tables and tables and mouths

soft of her cheek   turning away

green dark glare of television   small she
in a stranger's armchair   sharp hand pulls
the hair of her inattention   forced
and   refused hello

                    and goodbye at the garden

waist high cosmos, daisies   amber gone ash her
face, our eyes   cups of water   given given   held to
as the car pulls away   stabs of the white picket

                              soft she

                    shadow-lip murmurs
calm night room   night window   a moon if peace
were a face in sleep   placid brow   sweet dark hush
her lashes   smatter of freckles on
                         petals of her face

greasy white guy forcing his body against hers
bewildered   no   *please-no-not-this-again face*
                              dissembling
                         the opulent hotel
where everyone knows and says   nothing   flowers
         in oversized bouquets   cut fresh daily

                         turning away

three steps down to   earthen room   tang of decay
wasted flesh   skin and gone spirit
three dirt steps   always remaining between

                              us and the world

roomsfull of listening

a woman strong woman   her bandaged
         wrists and cropped head

who slips hard stones in my pocket   clear
         as our hearts   need to be

and a coil of her hair wrapped in cloth

                                        womanly

                                        untangled

         saved in my wicker box

                          humming

                          no

                          separations

         fevers beds and cloths to prepare the bodies of the dead

that room, low room   water murmurs and loam

your still-boned absence
                    to stay

the placid land above us, hard scape of blue sky

going on
         stay

in my arms   gravity and flesh

for your slack joints   hollow hollow skin-flute limbs

                                       stay

in your song thin going song   small

to my body my breathing my hands
                                    stay
as the tight summer hours   widened into

dusk

        stay

as the night-cloth rent

into stars in their falling
                  stay

light

         light

everyday with evil scouting out our infinite our most hidden beauty rigid I

am rigid

grief muslins   weft of loss   are granite

then rain drapes the window

sheaves of ample wet   sound the divide

all the casings tear

there   where my chest wants to move   my hands

and in the spaces:

curve of summer at midday's highest flight-songs and

i'm alright now, mom

sung low through water and treble-blue fractures of light

she, head bent, settles what is found into a silence, she, from that place where the river came through last winter

brilliant

unholdable: a year of birds and water

rain-closed days   hours at my window   hawk and crow

calling rough

hurling as stones against a meager sky

storm sparks

and words:

your letter's sheer tenderness that moved my bones   all the feathers

stashed

in their hollows   marrowing solid

an answer

whose stung half-lit hope   that in this way   no more may suffer, she a hummingbird

       late in arrival

       worrying air swift

              like that fleck in your eyes that said

                    tired or

                scared or

            closer

       your presence   still planet

       my own
            cutting on language from another life

       our silence   protective   fearful   waiting

          unnamed   *the body the energy field*   *she*

a woman   the stride of a whole day with her

loose-limbed now

                              easy tonight

under the last full moon of summer

breath

her blood   the flesh current

bass sweet   she

without a flinch a clutch of

muscle   she is

soft salt floes   russet

tempos   she is flaring

grace   from the bowl of her hips

frank

red

speech   she

is

this body for herself

                    whose vision feeds the pulse of our existences   *she*

a small brown bird in the house and I called out your name

    staunch her bundled feathers

        flex of eye   so like yours and I wanted

                to feed her

            something elemental

instead

wide the doors and windows   recalling

     your love of darkness   recalling

    your rare signs of flight across our northern field

  how from them I learned the birdness of my thick hands

               awkwardly

and   left to her going

      soft singing   moved a space of air

              and found me

   then wing sounds into rain   night   other places

   and words

   between us now like water   its flux and gesture   breaking

   soft   across the lips of islands

    upon whose labour   this   grinding   world   remains

a daughter

trusting the soft
radars of flesh, finds me
late

across the wall of my back
and sleep, she
finds me.

magnetic her tumble near
dishevel of limbs, her fiesty, kinetic head,
dips to kiss, her kiss on my breast -

        sweet apples so close

I waken -
our breathing is moon percussion
bones tenderly audible

and the room
a neat box of the world
apart from all that bridges us

in the dark and the blunt of my daughter's
naked touch
I waken

and ache

how unmake this we?

the sound of her voice root-breaking
was what I recognized
as if flayed from the sternum   a torn reed
her sound   splintered   bracing
then amber welling and soft sung prayers   will and desire
the sound of her
rising
rising
yellow
as dream-finch she cupped in her hand
head thrown and high   way back singing

                                      singing

to live

and hemmed in the sky's   elliptic
the sound of her breaking me wide
        horizon and backglance in shadow
moan of the bodies
weight of the blood without its tinder of pulse
stilled faces
                breath   flesh   felled
from the bones of hearts
                      into a river's forgiveness
                      the sound of her voice
reaching its grief-struck floor
and carrying

whose common knowledge language will not carry on its breath notes from deep to my surface self

placid limnal as a bone that might be passed
hand over hand to one whose
breath stirs a music songs a prayer

you had waited long for me

so many winters lain   in my marrow   waited

to sound.

mothers of the lost imagine ours as the one love-I wanted

you
and in the sleep-widened night and calm
so I would understand
you
and your other face   wrenched
in its last   gritting   *no*   against the voltage

daughter   the doorways of our worlds and our bodies are gone

we are each other's room

you   in all directions of my breathing

and I just here   breathing   trying my heart to sing this

After living in Vancouver for twelve years, **Oana Avasilichioaei** moved to Montreal where she completed an MA in writing and literature at Concordia University. Born in Romania, she is both tied to landscape and strangely detached, and often finds herself bewildered by the idea of "home." She now works in Montreal as poet, translator, editor and a part-time teacher at Dawson College. Some of her work has appeared in magazines such as *Prism International*, *Matrix*, *Grain*, *The Antigonish Review*, and anthologies *Running with Scissors* and *The Cyclops Review*. She is currently working on a long poem, *Hastings Park*, which draws its inspiration from the land and history, both real and imagined, of a Vancouver park.

Morgan Chojnacki's favourite early activities were reading stories and making them up. Family tales led her to complete an MA in Soviet and Eastern European Studies at Carleton University. She found her way to her own stories and graduated from The Writer's Studio at Simon Fraser University. Morgan's writing has appeared in *The Capilano Review*, *Emerge* and *Stories from the Button Jar*. The story in this anthology is excerpted from *The Book of Chapter One*, a manuscript that traces one woman's search for meaning, and the forces that lead her to confront her family's war-torn history.

Lindsay Diehl graduated in English Literature and History from the University of British Columbia; she also participated in *The Capilano Review*'s Writing Practices Program. She has been published by *Fireweed*, *Rant*, and *The Capilano Review* and was recently short-listed by *milieu* press in their emerging poet's manuscript contest. She currently lives on Commercial Drive with her cats, Earvin and Kobe, and her dog (who thinks he is a cat), Samson.

Marilyn Dumont's poetry has been widely anthologized in Canadian Literature. Her first collection, *A Really Good Brown Girl*, won the 1997 Gerald Lampert Memorial Award as well as Honourable Mention in the 1997 VanCity Book Prize while her second collection, *green girl dreams Mountains*, was awarded the 2001 Writer's Guild of Alberta's Poetry Award (Stephan G. Stephansson). Marilyn has worked as a university student advisor and administrator, a filmmaker and a sessional instructor. She holds a Master's in Creative Writing from UBC. She has also been Writer in Residence at the Universities of Alberta and Windsor and will be Writer in Residence at the University of Toronto for the 2004 Fall Term. She is presently working on a third collection of poetry, short fiction and a collection of personal reflections on the writing process.

Susan Andrews Grace's serial poem *Selah* investigates the world she imagines Plotinus, third century philosopher and Neo-Platonist, would have imagined Plato imagining. It sings Plotinus in the twenty-first century, with a Chinese echo from Confucius and Lao-tzu who were contemporaries of Plato. Sometimes poetry has the ability to be the reality when philosophy can only describe it. Her most recent book is *Ferry Woman's History of the World*, a three-book serial poem published by Coteau Books in 1998, which won the Saskatchewan Book of the Year. She teaches Creative Writing at Nelson Fine Art Centre in Nelson, BC.

sandra huber began writing at the age of 8, transcribing passages from Edgar Allan Poe books she found in her parents' library. Fascinated by the materiality and visual inscription of words, she crosses often into the visual arts with her highly aesthetic fabrication of language and the forms it's bound by. She is currently moving east to join six others chosen for the University of Toronto's first MA program in Creative Writing where she hopes to shape textilic poetry from a spool of ribbon. This is her first published poem.

Adeena Karasick (www.adeenakarasick.com) is a Canadian poet/cultural theorist, video and performance artist, as well as the award-winning author of five books of poetry and poetic theory, *The Arugula Fugues* (Zasterie Press, 2001), *Dyssemia Sleaze* (Talonbooks, 2000), *Genrecide* (Talonbooks, 1996), *Memewars* (Talonbooks, 1994), and *The Empress Has No Closure* (Talonbooks, 1992). Dedicated to the interplay of conflictual dialects, aesthetics, textures that impact on the construction of feminist and cultural identity, her articles, reviews and dialogues on contemporary poetry, poetics and cultural/semiotic theory are studied worldwide. She is Professor of Poetry and Critical Theory at St. John's University in New York.

Sarah Leavitt has published short fiction, comics and book reviews in *Geist* magazine. She graduated from The Writer's Studio at SFU in 2003, and will begin the MFA in Creative Writing at UBC in September 2004. *To The Birds* is a book-length manuscript-in-progress. Sarah is also a freelance writer and editor whose clients include publishing houses, non-profit agencies and educational institutions.

Sylvia Legris has published two poetry collections, *iridium seeds* (1998) and *circuitry of veins* (1996), both with Turnstone Press. Her work has appeared widely in journals, among them *The Malahat Review*, *The Capilano Review*, *Descant*, *Matrix*, *Grain*, *Contemporary Verse 2*, and, in the US, *Hayden's Ferry Review* and *Mid-American Review*. In 2001 she won *The Malahat Review* Long Poem Prize and she has twice been nominated for a Pushcart Prize.

Marcie McCauley's prose has won NOW's Feminist Fiction Writers' Award (US), and has been published in literary journals in Canada and England. She is equally passionate about writing and reading. www.marciemccauley.com

Lori McNulty turned to writing late in life at six years old, penning such classics as "The Mystery of the Golden Key," an entrancing tale about a girl who, shockingly, loses her key. Lori is currently completing a manuscript entitled *The Petrified Dancers* which depicts her trek to the sacred Garhwal Himalayas in India and the parallel journey of her mother's illness and dying. She holds an MA in English Literature from McGill University and is a graduate of The Writer's Studio at Simon Fraser University. Her writing has appeared in the *Globe & Mail*, *Trade* and *emerge*. Currently living and writing in Vancouver, she continues to misplace modifiers and house keys.

Christine Moore writes lyric prose. Her current project, *13 Resolute Road*, reflects on growing up in the United States 1971–72, during the Vietnam (and Cold) war(s). Her writing explores themes of violence, rigidity, control, perfection, and faith from the perspective of a child. Christine is a recent graduate of The Writer's Studio at Simon Fraser University. Her writing also appeared in the studio anthology, *emerge 2002*.

Translator, interpreter, teacher, community activist, award winning visual artist and acclaimed author of seven books, **Sarah Murphy** is the recipient of the 2003 Howard O'Hagan Award for her book of performance monologues, drawings and photomontage, *die tinkerbell die*, published by Spout Publications during an international residency with the Word Hoard in West Yorkshire in 2002. The present work is part of the *26 Nutmeg Mews* cycle of performance monologues of which *die tinkerbell die* is the first book-length publication. Other books include *The Forgotten Voices of Jane Dark*, *Connie Many Stories*, *Lilac in Leather* and *The Measure of Miranda*.

Shauna Paull is a mother, poet and community advocate. Since completing her MFA in Creative Writing at UBC, she has led writing workshops for youth and adults at the Shadbolt Centre for the Arts. In all things, Shauna works toward a world where women's poetry sings the fusion of political struggle and spiritual continuity and bridges us with our elders and our future. *notes from deep*, is an excerpt from an untitled work-in-progress.

Sharron Proulx-Turner is a Metis writer, educator and activist who grew to young adulthood in the Ottawa River valley and now lives and writes in Calgary. She is mother to three adult children, Graham, Barb and Adrian, and nokomis to Willow and Jessinia. Sharron has published a memoir, *Where The Rivers Join*, and a book of poetry, *what the auntys say*, and her work appears in five anthologies and several literary journals, including *Gatherings: The En'owkin Journal of First North American Peoples*, *absinthe*, *Tessera*, and *Prairie Fire*. *she walks for days inside a thousand eyes* is Sharron's second book of poetry.

Seema Shah lives in Vancouver, British Columbia. She is a physician and aspiring writer. Currently, she works as primary care physician in East Vancouver. Her poetry has been published in *West Coast Line* and *Crimson Feet: Poetry and Story*.

Meaghan Strimas was born and raised in Owen Sound, Ontario, and she has since resided in both Montreal and Toronto. Her work has been published in several Canadian journals which include: *CV2*, *The Harpweaver*, *Exile*, *The Existere* and *Signal*. She has recently completed her Creative Writing MA at Concordia University in Montreal, and her first collection of poetry, *Junk Man's Daughter*, will be published by Exile Editions in the fall of 2004. She shares an affinity with the writer Charles Simic, who says "Poems are other people's snapshots in which we recognize ourselves." Strimas is currently at work on her second collection of poetry, *Emblem*.

Nathalie Stephens writes in English and French and sometimes neither. Writing *l'entre-genre*, she is the author of several published works, including *Paper City* (Coach House, 2003), *Je Nathanaël* and *L'INJURE* (L'Hexagone, 2003 and 2004 respectively). She is the recipient of a 2002 Chalmers Arts Fellowship and a 2003 British Centre for Literary Translation Residential Bursary. Some of Stephens' work has been translated into Basque, Bulgarian, Portuguese and Slovene. She has translated Catherine Mavrikakis into

English and R.M. Vaughan into French. On occasion, she translates herself. She lives between.

Jennifer Still's poetry has appeared in Canadian journals including *The Fiddlehead, Prairie Fire, CV2, Other Voices, Qwerty, New West Review, tart* and *Spring.* A series of poems were dramatized for Globe Theatre's 2003 On the Line festival and another series will be broadcast on CBC radio in 2005. Jennifer's creative non-fiction has been broadcast on CBC radio and her poetry chapbook, *Remnant,* was published in 2002 by Jack Pine Press. She is the guest poet for the 2004 Sage Hill Teen Writing Experience. These poems are from her first manuscript, *Saltations.*

Rita Wong is the author of a book of poems, *monkeypuzzle* (Press Gang, 1998). She teaches at the Emily Carr Institute of Art and Design, and she lives in Vancouver. Her poems have been published widely in anthologies such as *Swallowing Clouds, Another Way to Dance,* and in journals such as *Fireweed, CV2, dANDdelion, Ms.* and *Prairie Fire.*

Onjana Yawnghwe was born in Thailand and now lives in Vancouver.

Sylvia Legris: "Nerve-Storms" reprinted by permission of the author. Nos. 1-6 appeared in *Contemporary Verse 2*, Vol. 23, No. 3 (Winter 2001), Nos. 7 and 8 appeared in *NeWest Review* (February 2001), and Nos. 1-8 appeared in *Mid-American Review*, Vol. 22, No. 1 (Fall 2001).

Shauna Paull: excerpts from this work-in-progress appeared in "from that place" in *xerography: the triple edition*, edited by Onjana Yawnghwe, Shane Plante, Travis V. Mason (Fish Magic Press, 2003). "a woman, the stride of a whole day" and "a daughter" appeared in *Atlantis: A Women's Studies Journal*, Volume 29.1 (Fall, 2004).

Meaghan Strimas: "Junk Man's Daughter" will be published by Exile Editions in the fall of 2004.

Rita Wong: "open the brutal" appeared in *Canadian Literature*, Issue 163 (Winter 1999). "storm," "take one," "ricochet," "reverb" and "cites of disturbance" appeared in *Prairie Fire* Annual, Volume 21, No. 4, (2001). "ricochet" also appeared in the "Lost in the Archives" issue of *Alphabet City*, No. 8, edited by Rebecca Comay (2002). "powell street" appeared in *Hot and Bothered 3: Short Short Fiction on Lesbian Desire*, edited by Karen X. Tulchinsky (Arsenal Pulp Press, Vancouver, 2001). "chaos feary" appeared in *Swallowing Clouds: An Anthology of Canadian-Chinese Poetry*, edited by Andy Quan and Jim Wong-Chu (Arsenal Pulp Press, Vancouver, 1999), and in *Ms. Magazine*, Vol. 10, No. 3 (April/May 2000). "damage" appeared in *Slant*, Vol. 1, No. 1, 2001. All these poems are reprinted by permission of the author.